KEYSTONE
CHRONICLES

Third Flatiron Anthologies
Volume 5, Book 17, Fall/Winter 2016

Edited by Juliana Rew
Cover Art by Keely Rew

Keystone Chronicles
Third Flatiron Anthologies
Volume 5, Fall/Winter 2016

Published by Third Flatiron Publishing
Juliana Rew, Editor and Publisher

Copyright 2016 Third Flatiron Publishing
ISBN #978-0692766712

Discover other titles by Third Flatiron:
(1) Over the Brink: Tales of Environmental Disaster
(2) A High Shrill Thump: War Stories
(3) Origins: Colliding Causalities
(4) Universe Horribilis
(5) Playing with Fire
(6) Lost Worlds, Retraced
(7) Redshifted: Martian Stories
(8) Astronomical Odds
(9) Master Minds
(10) Abbreviated Epics
(11) The Time It Happened
(12) Only Disconnect
(13) Ain't Superstitious
(14) Third Flatiron's Best of 2015
(15) It's Come to Our Attention
(16) Hyperpowers

License Notes

www.thirdflatiron.com

Contents

*****~~~~~*****

Editor's Note

by Juliana Rew

We're always amazed at how our authors take the theme we offer as a writing prompt and run with it. We had some unusually good writing this time, and that's saying a lot.

The prompt: We noted that a keystone is a central stone at the summit of an arch locking the whole together. It's something on which other things depend for support, the heart or core of something, the crux, or central principle. Welcome to *Keystone Chronicles*. This anthology features 19 stories, nearly a double issue, for this fall/winter. It's probably the most eclectic spec fic collection we've ever produced, even featuring a healthy dose of geological science.

Bursting out of the gate first is our lead story, "Our Problem Child: Langerfeld the Moon," by Marilyn K. Martin, who makes us appreciate how much we would miss that shiny silver disk in the sky if something ill were to befall it.

The idea of keystone species has become important as humans try to understand and preserve the natural environment. The Juno mission to Jupiter is giving us a closer glimpse of our solar system's gas giant. In "Hunt, Unrelenting," Sierra July writes an exciting, surrealistic story about what the keystone species of that planet might be.

Back on Earth, bees are a recognized keystone species, of course. But in the hands of author Judith Field, we're treated to an especially entertaining tale when magicians Pat and Mark form an alliance with our fuzzy friends to battle the UK version of Bigfoot.

Edward Palumbo channels Fredric Brown in his speculative story, "Desol 8," about an intergalactic travel reporter touring a new resort. We find we're not sure how we feel when that planet's key features are revealed.

Sometimes it's a matter of wanting something badly enough. But things get weird when slipstream/horror master A. P. Sessler's young lovers wish they'll never reach the end of "The White Picket Fence." Then it's a matter of perspective. Another excellently told tale, "Coding Haven" by Brandon Crilly, is the story of a coder who is key to saving the planet via virtual reality, but is not sure she can save herself.

Beware the end of the world? That old saw about there being a kook in every subway car gets a workout when expanded to an interstellar setting. John Marr really puts it out there in "Every Planet Has One." Bascomb James offers his ironic tale, "TANSTAAFL." Fans of Robert Heinlein might recognize the acronym, which stands for "there ain't no such thing as a free lunch."

We love time travel stories but can't abide anachronisms. Neither can Desmond Warzel, who pokes holes in the fun in "You Can Not Have a Meaningful Campaign If Strict Time Records Are Not Kept."

Space opera and movie lovers are sure to find something to their liking in John M. Campbell's thriller, "Keystone Mine," set in the Asteroid Belt.

Three authors give differing theories about how human civilization may have been given a boost by outside forces. UK writer Maureen Bowden shows how the Three Fates might have played a key role in raising up primitive humans in her tale, "Splinters." But others may beg to differ, as in Argentinian writer Gustavo Bondoni's fairy tale, "Racial Memory." And Bear Kosik's "See You on Hel," follows an overworked, underfunded uranologist who discovers extragalactic creatures have been helping humanity for millennia.

"To Their Wondering Eyes" by Sharon Diane King gives us a shot of steampunk fantasy, as stereographs spring to life and turn things inside out.

Editor's Note

We always enjoy switching things up by adding a bit of mythology and spirituality to the mix. In "How Far Away the Stars," Sri Lankan writer Sam Muller introduces us to a young knight determined to kill a dragon as the key to his reputation. (The dragon offers an alternative.) And Zerrin Ogtur presents us with a lovely parable of people gradually discovering their prophet to be the key to their uplift.

We close as usual with our "Grins and Gurgles" section, with flash humor pieces by Larry Lefkowitz ("Rejection"), Art Lasky ("I Should've Known Better"), and Damian Sheridan ("Remembrance of Saint Urho"). I'm still chuckling.

We hope you'll enjoy these chronicles, told by an international group of master storytellers.

*****~~~~~*****

Our Problem-Child: Langerfeld, the Moon

by Marilyn K. Martin

We are having problems with the Moon. Again. Well, the problems are mostly ongoing now, when they used to come in spurts during tidal stresses.

Wine glass in hand, I stood by our living room window and stared up at that dark lump in the sky. We'd bought this pre-war circular house on a hilltop because it could rotate 360 degrees, from grumpy grandchildren of the deceased builder, who could never get it to work right.

But my husband was brilliant at making pre-war machinery work. We'd only had a few temporary breakdowns in ten years. And we grew to love our little circular mountain top, since we could always see the Moon from any evening vantage point.

Our workdays never ended, since the RepRip wars. Our poor little orbital Moon had survived, but never again looked the same. Most of its outer mantle layer had been blasted away by oblique weapons-fire.

So, it was smaller and darker now. The semi-molten iron core was now fully solid, surrounded by mostly black basalt, hard and angular. The problem was trying to keep our smaller, denser Moon in a stable orbit.

Pinnard came in with a tankard of foamy beer. (I'd given him a craft beer hook-up to the local bar down below, as a Christmas gift a few years back.) "And what is our unruly stepchild doing tonight?" he sighed in only half-jest, as he sank into an easy chair facing the glass window I was standing beside.

That was the job of my husband and I, as the most senior PhDs in Astronomical Physics to survive the RepRip wars. The government begged us to figure out a stable orbit for the Moon—and then keep the sucker in orbit.

"Langerfeld took three laser-blasts in the past six hours, to push it back into orbit," I replied casually, checking my computer screen embedded in the upper corner of the glass window.

We called our geologic stepchild Langerfeld as an inside joke. Pinnard's last name was Feld, and we'd hidden out during the last RepRip war underground with his extended family. And his brother's youngest child, Langer, was singularly the most obnoxious, devious, unpredictable, and defiant child on the planet. Just like the Moon was now.

Pinnard stared out at the Moon now, frowning. "That's a lot of laser blasts for that small a time-frame," he offered, taking a sip of beer. "I see a little shimmy as it rotates. You still got a large warning-bumper on its permitted-zone-of-movement?"

"Always," I answered with a sigh. Pinnard was good at double-checking my stats without being obnoxious about it. Astronomy and Defense Techs had helped us work out the range of permitted orbital movement for the Moon. There was little chance it would drift away from Earth on its own, held by Earth's gravity and tidal forces. But if it inched too close to Earth, the defense-lasers on mountaintops blasted it back into orbit, before it could enter free fall and impact Earth.

It was tricky, but Public Debate polls had consistently shown that Earth's inhabitants didn't want the Moon destroyed. The older folks, especially, wanted the Moon left as it had been for millions of years: shining down on us in monthly cycles of curved slivers, plus that

12

monthly full moon of legend and lore. Guiding ancient farmers and growers who had lifted our ancestors out of the endless slog of following migrating herds of beasts to hunt for food, just to survive. And Congress agreed: Leave the Moon in orbit, as we all struggled to heal and rebuild.

Speaking of healing, I glanced back at the mural we'd painted together on the opposite wall, a mystical juxtaposition of farming families growing and harvesting food crops, with always an eye to the Moon and its silvery cycles. Agriculture tied to moon tables had finally let our ancestors settle down and start contemplating the mysteries of life, time, and space. Instead of tending to weeping children in damp caves, crying from hunger and cold—more than half of whom never lived to grow up.

No, no one wanted to lose our Moon. So, we sent away all the galactic mining companies who'd shown up after the truce was signed, offering to buy what was left of our Moon. For whatever its distance and remoteness, it was still part of us. Especially after the glowing-battles that destroyed the cities, and people had migrated out into overgrown rural areas to start cottage industries on a barter scale.

That hard and dark little shaky Moon became our talisman, part of a triangular touchstone including a benevolent Great God and a recovering Mother Earth. So, no, no one could fathom the thought of "losing" our Moon. *Someone* had to try and save it.

So, Pinnard and I spent our days—or, more accurately, our 24/7 lives—focused on keeping Langerfeld in orbit. We ran our stats constantly on some repaired computers, and communicated by phone with an odd assortment of Moon Tenders. We were now on a first-name basis with everyone from Pentagon generals to far-flung graduate students who tended the mountaintop defense lasers all over the world.

PHAZZ! The closest laser-correcter in the Rocky Mountains suddenly blasted out a white flash at the Moon, which shimmied as it was pushed back into orbit. I glanced at Pinnard, who shook his head. "I know," I admitted softly. "The data has been trending toward more laser-corrections more frequently, for several weeks now. I think it was caused by the meteor showers last month."

"I haven't told you," sighed Pinnard, putting his tankard of beer down on a side table, to rub his weary face. "But I've been taking a lot of heat from the Pentagon for the last few months."

I caught my breath and turned to focus on my husband. Without the correctional blasts from the defense lasers, we had no mission. And no Moon.

"Those laser blasts are getting more and more expensive," said Pinnard, looking up at me over clenched hands, like he always did when he was about to tell me something he knew I wasn't going to like.

"And we are tying up what are supposed to be planet-protecting defensive lasers," Pinnard continued. "It makes for. . . an exploitable weakness in our defense grid, according to General Dale.

"Since our mountaintop lasers are thousands of miles apart, all a clever enemy has to do is figure out what mountaintop laser will be deployed as the Moon starts to move closer to Earth in a tighter orbit. When that defense laser is blasting our Moon back into orbit, an enemy would have a doorway through our defense grid."

"And even with a truce," I added with a heavy sigh, "The Reps have no intention of vacating Mars."

Pinnard nodded grimly, and sat back to grab his tankard of beer. "It's the old Physics conundrum, my Love. The Law of Inevitability versus the Theory of Sustainment."

. . .

It was a calm and warm evening most places in America, in large-venue sports stadiums and outdoor starlight concert pavilions. Others watched live at home on TVs and monitors. The older folks tended to be tearful, like they were burying another loved one lost to the RepRip wars.

To the teens and 20s crowd, it was an exciting event with a hint of a party-time, although dancing and loud music were NOT allowed inside the venues. To younger kids in school, they'd spent the past week preparing for another holiday, learning the history amid crayon and crepe-paper crafts, and writing essays and poems.

At the appointed hour of 8 p.m. Eastern, the shrunken and shriveled, war-damaged orb in its full-Moon glory overhead in most of the U.S., the ceremony began. Pinnard and I sat on the dais at the Mall in Washington D.C. Suddenly the lights went out, and the live-television people were pointing fingers and gesturing with the precision of generals about to start a battle.

We stood quickly when they played the well-known Intro for the President of the United States. "The last time I stood on this dais, it was to announce a truce of the last RepRip War," he said. "Tonight, we say goodbye again, but for a more joyous occasion. For we shall now be able to feed and shelter every citizen, build roads and bridges, help businesses get back on their feet, and put this country back to work again."

There were more speeches and music, sonorous songs that echoed down the Mall, past war memorials and statues. Then, at precisely 9 p.m., there were more manic gestures and pointing from the long out-of-work, live-television people.

I swear I could feel the designated mountaintop lasers turn on, by the hum of serious vibrations through my feet. Pinnard already had one tear coming down his cheek as I reached for his hand.

"I am the last speaker," said a nervous 14-year-old now at the microphone. "Our Moon was kept steady in

15

orbit for as long as humanly possible, by my aunt and uncle. And they named it after me, as a private joke between them.

"I am Langer Feld. And they asked me to be the last speaker tonight, for a proper send-off of our only orbiting moon. And—" he quickly glanced over at Pinnard and me with a mischievous grin— "I've added a little surprise, to show them that I am capable of being responsibly attuned to the moment, and am no longer just an obnoxious toddler."

The orchestra played a short build-up, as Langer fiddled with cutting the strings attached to a tarp below the stage. As the four defense lasers suddenly blasted out of mountain tops many miles away, all around the City, a cascade of helium-filled balloons suddenly floated upward—obscuring everyone's view.

Pinnard leaned over. "Should we ever tell him that this is why they forbade fireworks on this occasion?" he asked sardonically.

"No," I sighed, catching one tear on my own cheek now. "Let the young people have their fun, Pinny. They'll never miss that old Moon like we do. It really shouldn't be a funeral for them, but a celebration. This country is going to experience massive improvements in all areas, and his generation will benefit the most. So. . . Langer got it right. Let the young people have their fun."

PHAZZ! The defense lasers connected with the Moon, and began to gently push it away, back, out of orbit. There were cheers and tears, people with lit candles, everyone waving goodbye.

As the Moon got smaller and smaller in the distance, dark machinery craft suddenly appeared around it in space. Amid flashes, they attached tractor-beams to the remnant of our Moon, that hard little ball of basalt and high-grade iron that tended toward steel—and was very valuable. They started towing it away, out of our solar system.

About the Author

Marilyn K. Martin is a freelance genre author and humorist. She is focusing now on science fiction short stories, with a little fantasy, horror, and paranormal thrown in to keep things interesting.

She had a steampunk Western story appear in *Steampunk: The Other Worlds in 2015* (Villainous Press). A Canadian publisher then bought the reprint rights, and published it on Amazon as a Short Read, which continues to sell well. They also published it in their anthology with other Short Reads, *Cosmic Hooey.*

She has other genre books available on Amazon, including her high-tech humor book, *The Best Computer Humor On The Web.*

Marilyn's also had short stories published in *Fiction Vortex* magazine and the anthology, *Strange Valentines* (sold thru Lulu), which won small awards. Look for other of her short stories in *Perihelion SF, Deadman's Tome, Encounters,* and *Cosmic Crime.*

*****~~~~~*****

Hunt, Unrelenting

by Sierra July

Mouton bothers over his troublesome hair, preening, preparing it for the Leopards. His hair (fleece, rather) is his only guard. He flares his nostrils, irritated with its incorporation, shelters among his herd just in case, awaiting his triumph or demise. His mother and brother's cores tremble beside him. He can sense them. The Cloud Leopards are descending.

They give Jupiter its splotch of color, the Cloud Leopards of the Great Red Spot. Yes, the blood patch of Jupiter, a place of little to no substance, a place one couldn't put his or her feet on, but a vital locale all the same. But color isn't the only service the Leopards provide the Spot; they also hunt the Sheep who likewise call the Spot home, their natural prey. The Sheep's fleece shivers under pressure, colorless as air and just as light. They keep their Planet adrift, running (floating) round and round, providing spin, and gas from their exhausted lungs. They are gas, all of them, Leopard and Sheep and Planet. But Greed consumes the Leopards.

A younger Sheep paces in fright, his eyes bulging and his tongue lolling. Mouton makes his way to him and leads him to the center of the herd with his family. The clouds around them change. They are coming.

The Leopards are a mass of swirling smoke, dotted with the red that gives the Spot its name. They are also a crowd of teeth and claw, sharpened daggers just as red as their pelts but red for other reasons. Their pelts paint the Spot, and the blood of Sheep paints their built-in weapons. Many Sheep have fallen under the swipe of a paw or under the crunch of jaws. Blood should cover their land, dripping and spreading and drowning out the neutral shades, but that's where the Sheep's fleece comes in handy.

Mouton watches the hairs on his back from the corner of his eye, waiting for them to run red.

Wool thick and burly absorbs misery, takes on shades of Death momentarily. With blood attempting to weigh them down, Sheep keep running, scattering their brethren's particles into empty space. A process labeled Grazing, scraping the old off and away for a glimpse of the new. It's how their home remains neutral, a balance of two forces, predator and prey, light and dark. When balance is upset, Sheep lose their vision, and light and dark look very much the same.

That day, again, has come, and Mouton has to brace himself to keeping from racing.

...

Leopard Greed has taken out a sizable chunk of the Sheep's herd. Jupiter is running red, a tinge darker than blood. It's a color unrecognizable to Sheep, dark like misery but with a smell (or a ghost of one, since scents have no place in space), rotten. To eyes other than Sheep's, burgundy laced in black and allowed to simmer into a single entity, it has the look and texture of a throbbing heart. Scientists gazing into telescopes would see two red planets side by side, Mars and Jupiter, the angry eyes of God.

On Earth, malice and determination leave from a man with black intentions. Others like him, tormenters and thieves are also robbed of purpose, from Venus, Earth, Mars, and Saturn, two-legged Humans and six-tentacle-armed aliens alike. . . temporarily. The Leopards are Feeding.

Hunt, Unrelenting

Key to Leopards is Absorption. The Draining lasts a good minute (a minute for the Hunt; a minute of cleanliness and indecision to those robbed), and only the best of Hunters can gather the energy to make kills. The sloppy, the slow, go hungry, starve with one miss, then carry on dispersion same as the Sheep's fallen, mist into emptiness. Ashes to ashes, cloud to cloud. Like dust particles given to wind, they float back whence they came.

What set off the Hunger? No Sheep, Leopard, or outsider knows for sure. Could be a blip in the Leopards' judgments, the same that they invoke in surrounding organisms, aliens being forced to give up their rationale; it could be plain and simple Greed.

Sheep meat is sweet, the Leopards would proclaim, sweet, sweet, addictively sweet.

Then again, it could just be Madness.

The reflection of Jupiter's moons in their eyes, the Leopards stalk the Sheep. Desire to stay inside the boundaries of the Red Spot depleted, Leopards roam where they please. All is red now anyhow. Paws padding soft (on cloud), spreading wide like snowshoes with each step, they sneak. Utilizing camouflage, transparent pelts blending into vapor, spots mimicking craters, they lurk, ready to pounce.

…

Eclipsed by the fallen, Mouton's fleece has changed, converted into razor wire on guard, quivering silver laces itching to slice. Leopards have mouths to parry this, palates of iron, but they'd have to find him first. He tries to ignore the remaining hint of his brother who'd sprinted from safety, already dispersing into the atmosphere. His eyes cloud as he huddles closer and closer still to the thinning herd. He finally closes them, trying to put himself in another place and time, but his mother's bleats ground him.

…

Away on Earth, again, Scientists are studying, contemplating the strange conundrum confounding one of their treasured planets.

"That is Jupiter, right?" One spectacled man says to another, stuffing his eye against his telescopes eyepiece, so that it leaves an impression when he pulls away.

"It is," the other answers after close observation, "but it. . . looks red."

"That it does, but why?"

. . .

The Leopards thirst for sweet meat, more than their mouths can load, more than their stomachs can hold. The Sheep's quivering is heard as bells, the jingle of wind chimes speaking to a breeze.

The Sheep stand their ground, their eyes shining yellow in nonexistent light, watching their enemies' eyes glow red. And then began another wave of attacks.

Again, Sheep on the outskirts are attacked first, clawed and bitten, brought down, dead. Red molecules make their way into the surviving Sheep's fleece, collecting against barbed wire as if their defenses have already been put to use. Those molecules are charging the wire, electrifying it with an energy all their own. The Sheep can feel it, tingling into their pores and fueling their unrelenting guard. Their wires have new power, stronger power than Greed; the chorus sung by brave individuals in order to warn their clan of danger, the call that gets those brave individuals slaughtered for the sake of the young, the old, and the weak. The young Mouton cowers among them.

The new power pulses, singes the Leopards' eyes like coals placed in their eye sockets; it's so bright, it slays some of their advances, but not all. Fire cannot squelch fire, only intensify the flame, and that's what the Sheep are unintentionally doing, dousing flame in oil, adding Hate to the Leopards' Hate. And angry cats have a way of lashing out, uncaring who the offender, if rubbed the wrong way.

A Leopard leaps on Mouton. He whips his head away, pushes his wired frame forward. A yowl escapes the cat, and it drops away. Mouton searches for Mother, finds her still cowering. He can no longer see the lost and panicked youngster. He bounds for his mother, makes it too late. She's snatched, ripped, broken. Mouton crumbles, momentarily stunned, and then looks on the other shattered faces among the Sheep, exhausted but not defeated. The defiant are regrouping to the center. Mouton joins them.

The Sheep in the center remain glazed with grief, painted with it, their hooves touching nothing but cloud cover grown heavy. Rather than going on the offensive in a clash they know they couldn't win, wire versus teeth, claws, speed, stamina, they come up with a new technique, thought up at the spur of the moment out of desperation.

The move that preserves the Sheep, preserves Jupiter's identity, is the Tip.

Utilized by a select few of Earth's animals, the technique has its own distinct name—playing possum, an art that has saved many a life. Played even by Humans for laziness, immaturity, or boredom, feigning Sleep or Death, the procedure is basic and the result is counter to an animal that loves the thrill of the chase, the life draining from the eyes like jelly.

Sheep spongy with the smell of decay topple over with their stiff legs in the air. Death snuggles against them, but at the instant of their Tipping their coats are still razor sharp, gleaming, glistening. The Leopards reap confusion, puzzlement inking them, blotting out the red. Greed dies; Hunger is parried, quenched only by the little sweet meat their tongues succeeded in savoring. It is when the Leopards return to their domain, the Spot they light with their spots, that the Sheep end their charade, and run.

They run (fly) and run (float) until they are made of cloud again, until their coats are white again, Mouton, swiftest of all.

Jupiter goes from being a second red planet to itself, enters back into its neutral corner.

Aliens (Martians, Venetians, Saturnians, and the like) see a planet not worth invading, so bland is the color (all but the Spot that speaks Death like a promise), and Earthlings, Earthen Animals and Man, see no longer the Anger in God's eyes, they see a face malevolent and strong, a red-eyed creature with the courtesy to wink. None see the Leopards, the Sheep, the turmoil, the resolve. But isn't that always how it is? The mayhem is swept under the rug (space vacuumed) but not forgotten, not really.

Nature can't take care of the Leopard population, their overgrowth, their abundance. But something else does, some other natural force, unseen but resilient. Leopards plagued by Greed lose their spots, the very essence of their being. Ghostly pale and naked of pattern, they crumple and spasm into hot spray rather than cloud, the embodiment of stardust. Their particles mingle and collect to form blinking orbs of light hot enough to burn, cool enough to keep wishes tucked inside where they can stay on fire and not melt away. They are the start of a new era, a fresh galaxy. Other Leopards live on, as always, Absorbing Hate and Anger, if for a minute, and converting them into usable energy, energy for the Hunt.

Still, there are a handful of Sheep that can't Tip, don't have it in them. They seek adventure, the breath of Death right in their faces. Some desire to be resuscitated by it, desire Death huffing into their lungs so that they may feel more alive (regardless of how ironic it sounds). They are the risk takers, the daredevils, juvenile or downright stupid; they are the Hunted, and now Mouton watches over them.

24

About the Author

Sierra July is a University of Florida graduate, writer, and poet. Her fiction has appeared in *Robot and Raygun, T. Gene Davis's Speculative Blog,* and *SpeckLit,* among other places, including Belladonna Publishing's *Strange Little Girls* anthology.

*****~~~~*****

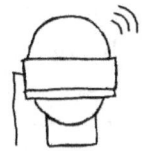

Coding Haven

by Brandon Crilly

There was a perfect field in existence.

Like millions of similar fields across Haven, the grass was straight and brilliantly green. Randomized trees offered the right amount of shade; the sky overhead was bright blue, peppered with natural white clouds. Being springtime, the sun wasn't too hot, and the breeze was cool and pleasant. There was also plenty of space for the people choosing to enjoy a day outdoors, with picnics or bicycling or a dozen other activities.

In an isolated corner of the field, five people stood around a single tree. None of them said a word. The tree, an eight-foot poplar still on its way to full adulthood, stood unchanged for several minutes.

And then it flickered again.

It was only for a moment, so rapid that if one wasn't watching they would likely miss it. Crouched at the base of the tree, Orianna Dever knew they were lucky the phasing was so quick; hopefully it would be a while before anyone else noticed.

She let out a quiet of sigh of defeat.

"So, the warehouse wasn't an isolated incident, then," Lionel McAllister said behind her. He was standing slightly back from the others, in his trim suit, unconsciously aloof as always.

"No."

A few days ago, they had gone out to a warehouse on the outskirts of recreated Philadelphia. Someone found an exterior wall covered in grass, as though someone had rotated the ground ninety degrees. The grass looked alive, even shivered in the breeze—but it was supposed to, of course.

"You said the warehouse might have been a coding error, correct?" Lionel asked. "Or possibly data corruption."

"Yes."

"So what does *this* mean?"

"Not sure," Orianna said slowly. "It might be dying."

"*What's* dying?" Lionel suddenly sounded panicked. "The bloody tree is dying?"

"She's just being melodramatic," Emalee Jacobs said from the other side of the poplar, where she was studying its leaves. "It can't die. It's just another glitch."

Ever the optimist, kiddo, Orianna thought. She still couldn't help calling her assistant "kiddo," even though Emalee was in her late twenties. There was something about the pretty blonde and her innocent personality that made her seem like she had just graduated high school.

"Are there supposed to be glitches, Ory?"

Orianna looked up to meet Saan Kalpana's gaze. She tried to keep her eyes neutral, but when she saw her mentor's jaw tighten, she knew that she'd failed.

A rough-hewed hand touched her shoulder. Orianna didn't look at her husband, Will, not wanting to worry him, too. He'd always been able to read her, even here in Haven.

"So what do we do now?" he asked her.

Orianna softly chewed the inside of her cheek. She wanted to reassure the others, tell them that she would figure out exactly what was happening and how to fix it. In her gut, though, she already knew what was happening.

The trick now was to figure out how to lie to the people she cared about most.

There aren't supposed to be any glitches. The code, the construct, it was all supposed to be perfect. There can't be any glitches.

You should have asphyxiated yourself when you had the chance.

She stared at her hands, pretending that the others weren't waiting for her to answer Will's question. They looked so real to her. When she had written the code for her own consciousness, she had decided to include the faint scars on her wrists from Attempt Number One. Most other people had opted to erase evidence of past trauma, but Orianna hadn't even considered it. The scars were so much a part of her that she couldn't envision her body without them.

When an interminable amount of time had almost passed, she said, "It's probably nothing."

And immediately she knew that she had failed again. She heard Will's slight exhale of breath, like he used to do before heading back to base to meet a new batch of recruits. She looked up and saw Emalee's eyes drop. Lionel actually crossed his arms and wandered away, tapping dandelions with his shoes.

They knew her better than she knew them. She knew math and code, not people. When it came to people, she always screwed up sooner or later. It amazed her sometimes that Will still loved her, how he actually found her inability to communicate endearing.

Orianna looked around at the others—the people who had made Haven possible. *If ever there was a stranger combination of partners*, she thought. Emalee, the genius graduate student who still believed in fairies. Saan, whose calm approach made him a trusted advisor to not one, but several world leaders. Lionel, the ambitious venture capitalist, but also first to criticize anything he didn't understand. Will, who could boom commands at recruits but barely spoke in a group of his peers.

And me. The maniac that convinced everyone they could escape the end of the world.

We didn't escape it. We just switched to a different ending.

"I should brief the Prime Minister about this," Saan said.

"Saan, you really don't need to." Orianna thought about having to lie to everyone who had supported her when she first proposed the Upload, but Saan raised a hand.

"Just so he's prepared in case any more glitches arise. I'll tell him you're looking into it."

"You still call him the Prime Minister, even here?" Will said.

"Force of habit, I suppose." Saan shrugged. "It's never felt right to call him Paul."

As Saan walked away to make his call, Will squeezed Orianna's hand. "You'll figure this out, Ory."

She nodded to appease him. His encouragement couldn't overcome her doubt. On some level, she had always known the Upload wouldn't work.

The tree flickered again. Orianna marveled at the universe's cruelty, that it was choosing now to prove she was a failure.

"I'm gonna go check on Hannah," Will said. "Give you and Emalee some time to think."

He kissed her on the cheek and was gone. Lionel muttered something about the millions he had sunk into their project, but when he realized no one was listening he wandered away again.

Emalee came over to her. "Any ideas on where to start?"

Jumping off a cliff. That would be Attempt Number Three, after her wrists and the car exhaust. *Too bad it won't work.*

Coding Haven

Everyone knew that nothing could really change in Haven. The code created a permanent universe. It could be manipulated, in the same way that you could pick up a rock and crush it in an old VR program. But there was no injury, no death, and no birth.

"I just need to think for a bit, Em. I'll let you know."

...

They discussed a variety of options. Haven's code could be accessed from inside the program, but there were a million places just to start searching for the problem. It was the most sophisticated program ever conceived, which made the task of saving it seem impossible. And there was always the possibility that something had gone wrong with the hardware in the real world, which they couldn't access.

Eventually Orianna got tired of discussing it, told Emalee she wanted to run through some options on her own, and went home. The sky was starting to get dark as she sat in her office, staring at the screen floating in the center of the room. Lines of code crawled past, all of it recognizable and familiar, but none of it telling her what needed to be done.

She swiveled her old, wooden chair around so she was gazing out the office window. Will was down there, running around their backyard with Hannah. As she watched, he scooped Hannah up into his arms and spun her around in a circle. Orianna smiled at her cry of joy—at the little girl with her mother's short, dark hair and her father's stubbornness, just the way she had always been.

Not for the first time, she wondered what would happen to Hannah, when Haven ultimately broke down. The thought of her daughter flickering like the poplar filled her with dread.

She had closed the screen showing Haven's code by the time Will came to check on her. He gently massaged her shoulders while she stared at the wall,

31

envisioning puffy white clouds dropping from the sky and trees made out of fractal cubes.

"We should go somewhere."

"Where do you want to go?" Will asked, slightly puzzled.

"I don't know. Cairo. I always meant to take a trip there before the Upload. I think it's pretty much the same now."

"Shouldn't you be focusing on your work?"

"I don't know if there's anything I can do."

He didn't say anything for a very long time. The pressure of his hands never changed, despite the thoughts that she knew must be whirring through his mind. Or maybe, she wondered, he didn't worry nearly as much as she thought he did. *When have I ever understood people?*

"You'll figure it out, Ory," he said again.

And Orianna had to try her damnedest not to scream.

...

In the end, as expected, she didn't figure it out.

But Emalee did.

Staring at the code, watching her genius assistant manipulate fragments and rework algorithms, Orianna could barely believe the simplicity of the solution. Emalee's face was a mask of calm as she worked. Only when the first rays of a smile spread across her face did it become clear to Orianna that she was done.

The kiddo had just saved the world.

"I have to reboot the system," Emalee explained. "It'll just be for a moment. I figure most people won't notice, but Saan said he's going to issue a statement anyway. Then we'll see if the correction works."

They were sitting side-by-side in front of the poplar. It was phasing about every ten seconds now, sometimes reappearing with extra branches or disconnected limbs. The field was deserted, as though people were afraid of the corruption spreading to them and their loved ones. Once the reboot was complete, someone would stay in the field for a while and watch the poplar, just to be sure.

You did it, kiddo. Because I couldn't. They had called Orianna the savior of humanity when she first proposed the Upload and proved that it could be constructed. Keep the collective human consciousness alive, and give the real world a chance to save itself from the damage that had been done to it. *And everyone almost died anyway.*

"I need you to do something else to the code."

"What? Do you think I missed something?"

Orianna snorted. "No, you got it perfectly right. This is something else."

"What?"

Orianna told her. It was something she had considered before, but didn't have the courage to try. But Emalee's success made it clear that Haven no longer needed her. Orianna felt her family would be better off without her. And at the very least it was an ironic way for her to go.

Emalee shook her head, flat out refused, and then tried to threaten her friend. Orianna didn't budge. And eventually Emalee agreed.

Nothing could be created or destroyed in Haven, just manipulated. Except if the code was rewritten and the system was rebooted. Then, Orianna knew, anything was possible.

...

When Orianna opened her eyes sometime later, she wondered if there was actually an afterlife that she was keeping all of humanity from visiting.

And then she realized: Emalee hadn't made the changes she had asked for.

The sun was shining above her, and as usual the sky was blue with the perfect scattering of clouds. Birds were chirping in the distance. When she turned her head, she saw vibrantly green grass swaying in the wind, surrounded by a wrought iron fence and a band of bright wildflowers.

It wasn't her home. But it was as close to her home as possible.

Will appeared beside her, his worried smile a familiar sight. He sat down on the chair beside her and didn't say anything for a very long time.

"You tried again."

"Yeah."

"You can't blame yourself for what happened."

Of course I can. I'm the brilliant Doctor Dever, remember? I'm supposed to have all the answers.

"I didn't think you were still looking for a way out," Will said.

"There isn't one, now." As usual, she knew the remark was not the right thing to say. It seemed to bother her less and less.

Will didn't get angry with her. He knew her too well, and loved her too much.

"Then we're just going to have to work on it," he said, and went back to watching the clouds.

About the Author

An Ottawa teacher by day, Brandon Crilly has been published in *On Spec*, *Nonlocal Science Fiction*, and other markets. He was a Semi-Finalist in the 4th quarter of Writers of the Future 32. You can find Brandon at brandoncrilly.wordpress.com or on Twitter: @B_Crilly.

*****~~~~~*****

Splinters

by Maureen Bowden

The Three Fates sat around their kitchen table drinking afternoon tea. Their bijou abode was located in the unfashionable quarter of the Immortal Realm. With a few exceptions, the sisters didn't socialise with the gods and their promiscuous offspring. They preferred their own company.

"Put the kettle on, Clo," Sissie said. "Lets have a fresh brew. This one's stewed."

"And open a packet of ginger hobnobs," Possie said. "I fancy a dunk."

Sissie glared at her over her bargain basement reading spectacles. "You'll get fat. Too many dunked hobnobs and insufficient exercise is a recipe for disaster."

"Don't fuss, Sissie," Clo said. "Let her dunk all she likes. It's not as if she can die, is it?"

"That's not the point. It's a matter of keeping up standards."

While Clo and Sissie were squabbling over her fitness regime, Possie was staring at the globe that was perched alongside the sugar bowl, and strategically placed to cover a gravy stain on the tablecloth. It was the sisters' universal viewfinder. "Shut up, you two and take a look at this."

"Not another supernova is it?" Sissie said. "When you've seen seventeen million you've seen them all."

"This is much more fun. Something's occurring on that pretty little blue planet, the one with the atmosphere."

They hovered around the globe and Possie pressed the 'zoom in' button. On the blue planet, tiny, fishlike creatures were crawling out of the ocean. Sissie said, "They've grown legs. They're evolving."

Clo shouted, "Yay," and punched the air. "I knew that planet had attitude."

Possie dunked a hobnob into her fresh cup of tea, swallowed the chunk of ginger flavoured mush, and burped. "They've a long away to go, and they'll need our help."

Late into the night they watched, as time sped by on the blue planet and dinosaurs roamed the continents.

"These things are going nowhere, evolution-wise," Clo said. "Life's too easy for them. They've become complacent."

Sissie said, "You're right, Clo, they have a false sense of security, and the other species aren't getting a chance, with the big pea-brains lording it over them. What do you think, Possie?"

"They're a dead end. Chuck an asteroid at them, and we'll see what happens tomorrow."

Next morning, the sisters zoomed in on the blue planet while they ate their breakfast.

"Those hairy things swinging in the trees look promising," Clo said. "I'll spin a thread of intelligent life for them."

Sissie said, "I'll measure it. We don't want them living too long. Fast, short, and sweet is best."

Possie took a knife out of the cutlery drawer. "And when they've had their span, I'll cut the thread and they'll drop out of the tree."

"We need to stop them getting stuck, like the pea-brains," Clo said. "If they have too much brute strength they won't need to be clever, so I'll give them frailty."

Sissie said, "They'll have to learn to overcome problems, so I'll give them adversity. What about you, Possie?"

"Don't know yet." She chewed her buttered toast, and slurped her tea. "I need to have a word with Prometheus. He has a good imagination."

"That boy's trouble," Clo said. "Don't invite him back here."

Possie laced up her sensible shoes and trotted along to the Speakeasy where the Titans and other young immortals hung out. The sign above the door read, "Hephaestus's Hideaway." *Doesn't exactly trip off the tongue*, she thought.

Prometheus was leaning against the bar with a pint glass of nectar in one hand and a nymph in the other. He beckoned to her. "Mixing with the rabble, Possie? Come and have a drink."

"The Fates never touch the stuff, laddie. I need a word, in private, if you don't mind."

He nibbled the nymph's ear. "See you later, Hesione."

"Make it quick, big boy." She winked at Possie, sashayed across to the musicians' corner, and draped her arms around Orpheus, who ignored her and carried on harping.

"I'm all yours, Lady Fate," Prometheus said, leading her to an empty table and pulling out a chair.

"Of course you are, big boy." She sat down. "This won't take long. My sisters and I have found a planet with sentient life that has the potential for higher intelligence."

He laughed. "So, the humans are about to show up at last."

"Humans?"

"That's what I call them."

"How do you know about them?"

"I guessed."

"That's what I like about you, Prom. You have imagination."

"So, how can I help?"

"Tell me how I can motivate them into making the effort."

"You need a keystone." He clicked his fingers, summoning the waiter, and passed him his empty glass. "Fill it up." He turned back to Possie. "Are you sure you won't join me?"

"Positive. Can we get back to the keystone? Where do I get it?"

He delved into the pocket of his breeches and produced an oval, crystalline pebble. The colours of the spectrum danced and swirled beneath its surface. "Throw it to them," he said. "Shatter it into fragments. They'll breathe it, bathe in it, and absorb it into their spirit. It'll focus their minds and feed their sense of purpose, lead them into great danger, but bring them prosperity. Without it, they'll stagnate and become extinct."

"Pretty speech," she said, taking the pebble into her hands. It felt warm. "What is it?"

"It's—"

"Wait," she interrupted. The clientele were closing in around them, taking an interest in their conversation. "I don't like this mob knowing my business. Whisper it."

He leaned close to her ear, and told her the keystone's name.

She smiled. "Thank you. That should do it."

He escorted her to the door. "You know, Possie, you should get out more. You're a fine looking manifestation, but you don't make the best of yourself, and a sedentary lifestyle piles on the weight. Get Aphrodite to give you a make-over."

"What, and have this crowd trying to rip off my corset? No thanks. I'd rather stay frumpy and keep my dignity."

He laughed and hugged her.

38

Before she left, she said, "A word of advice, Prom: Don't upset Zeus, he bears a grudge. You need to hang on to your liver."

"I appreciate the warning, Lady Fate, but I live in the moment, and right now I'm more interested in hanging on to Hesione."

Possie fought back a momentary envy of the youngsters and their wild ways. *It always ends in tears,* she reminded herself, as she trudged back home. After slumping back in her chair at the kitchen table, she unlaced her shoes.

"My feet are killing me. Put the kettle on, Clo, and make mine coffee. I need a burst of caffeine." She took the keystone out of her purse. It warmed her palm.

"What's that?" Sissie said.

"Caffeine first, then I'll fill you in."

She told them everything, except what Prometheus had whispered in her ear.

"Right," Clo said. "We know what it can do, according to a precocious young Titan with more ambition than sense, but what, exactly, is it?"

"I'll leave that for the two of you to figure out. I'm just a lazy old biddy who sits on her backside getting fat. Show me how smart you are."

...

The sisters zoomed in on the blue planet. The hairy things were leaving the trees and sheltering in caves. Possie threw the pebble. It soared through the atmosphere and shattered. An exploding rainbow covered the oceans and landmasses with fine grains of colour. Larger fragments, splinters of solid light, continued to circle the planet.

One of the larger splinters struck a cave dweller. He turned his face towards the sky, basking in the sun's warmth. A cloudbank brought a sudden chill, and the primitive human rubbed his arms, generating heat. His companions watched and copied. He picked up two sticks

39

and repeated the rubbing action. A flame burst into life, and his companions held their hands towards it, withdrawing them when the fire scorched their fingertips.

"I believe we've witnessed a step in human evolution," Possie said, "and it was the keystone splinter that instigated it."

Clo nodded. "The humans that those things perforate will be special. They'll become the keystone's living hosts, and take the species forward."

She was right. Through the ages, each time a splinter struck, a special human emerged: Socrates, Pythagoras, Hipparchia, Aspasia, Charles Darwin, Marie Curie, Albert Einstein, Edwin Hubble, Rosalind Franklin, Jocelyn Bell Burnell, and many more.

"What is it, Possie?" Sissie said. We can't work it out. Tell us what the keystone really is."

Possie sighed, "Enough. Stop pecking. I'll tell you next time we get a special one, but right now I need a snooze. The caffeine's worn off."

She slept, and dreamed about the blue planet's children. She wept over their moments of madness: the persecutions, oppressions, and genocides, and she cheered for the noble spirit that shone through, as humankind, driven by the keystone, observed, investigated, learned, and secured its survival.

Sissie's voice hauled her out of the dream. "Possie, wake up. Another one's caught a keystone splinter. This time you have to tell us what it is."

She stifled a snore, opened her eyes, and stretched. "Alright, I'm coming. Let's take a peek at the latest clever clogs."

The Three Fates looked upon the child called Stephen Hawking, and they blessed him:

Clotho, The Spinner, his life's thread emerging from her wheel, "I bring Frailty, that he discovers true strength."

Splinters

Lachesis, the Measurer, determining the span of his days, "I bring Adversity, that he strives to overcome."

Atropos, The Cutter, "I bring the greatest gift, Curiosity, that he finds his answers before I wield my knife."

About the Author

Maureen Bowden is a Liverpudlian, living with her musician husband in North Wales, where they try in vain to evade the onslaught of their children and grandchildren. She has had sixty-eight stories and poems accepted for publication by paying markets, including *Grievous Angel, Third Flatiron, Alban Lake, Mad Scientist Journal*, and *Unsettling Wonder,* among others. Silver Pen publishers nominated one of her stories for the 2015 international Pushcart Prize.

She also writes song lyrics, mostly comic political satire, set to traditional melodies. Her husband has performed these in Folk clubs throughout England and Wales.

Maureen recently retired from a long career with Her Majesty's Revenue and Customs, and in 2013 she obtained a First Class Honours Degree from the Open University. As well as Literature and History, the Degree included modules in Creative Writing and Advanced Creative Writing. She achieved a distinction in both.

She loves her family and friends, Rock 'n' Roll, Shakespeare, and cats.

*****~~~~~*****

Desol 8

by Edward Palumbo

"Coffee for you, Mr. Quest?" Grace asked. "We have a good blend here, especially reserved for visitors like yourself."

"No, thank you, I just need a nap, with your permission. Where should I set up?"

She came around her desk and motioned for me to follow her. "We have a suite for you in the J Wing. The J Wing is for VIPs."

"I hardly consider myself that," I responded, "but thank you for the kind words."

Grace was a pale sort and on the tall side. She was a female of her species and not measurably dissimilar to the females on my home planet. She wore a silver uniform, and her forehead was marked by a green cross. I followed her down the bright hall. She set a brisk pace. The suite was all I could have expected, large, well equipped, and complete with a soft bed I enjoyed for ten hours.

...

The president of Desol 8, Horace Whitley, requested my visit after I had finished breakfast, and I was happy to oblige. Horace was a tiny little man and likely more ancient than every antique in his office, or what I assumed to be antiques.

"You are a journalist?" he asked, as I took a seat at his desk.

"Yes, sir," I promised.

"Then, asking you the mechanical details of the vessel you arrived upon may be fruitless."

"Yes," I agreed, "fruitless. Captain Bayles can help you with details, from a scientific standpoint. I am hardly a scientist, but I am a darn fine reporter."

"I don't doubt you. Your vessel, that is to say, the one that brought you here, what do you call it?"

"The Inspired."

"A fine name. So far as you know, it is in good working order, after your long trip?"

"Yes, I would say we need nothing more than a proper tune up."

Horace laughed at the phrase. "I have not heard the term *tune up* before."

"I didn't think you would have, sir. As I have said, despite all the light-speed travel I have under my belt, I am a journalist, not a scientist."

"Even journalists may have their moments," he laughed. "I have some free insight for you, insight I learned when I studied the cosmos as a student: the speed of light only has meaning where there is time. Without time, there is no speed. If time has stopped, or, better said, slowed to the point when it is hardly measurable, you can go anywhere almost instantly, because everything happens almost instantly."

"And how does one slow down time?" I asked Horace.

"By speeding up," he said, after he adjusted his glasses, "if you move quickly enough, time barely moves at all."

"I'll remember that."

"Good. Many a man before you has forgotten this concept and has mistakenly traveled into the distant future *or* the distant past without a clue. Those can be cold places, particularly as you would likely not be acquainted with anyone."

...

I did not ask Grace her age, but were she from my hometown, she would have been about thirty and, therefore, ten years younger than myself. Whatever her age, thirty, or two-thousand thirty, she was cordial and brilliant, and entirely receptive to my visit.

"Four years ago," she said, "Horace appointed me the intergalactic, public relations manager for Desol 8. I enjoy my job, and I enjoy meeting new people and helping them, and I am happy to help you with your article in any way I can."

"Thank you," I said, "I will have an awful lot of questions."

Our ground-transport was a carbon-fiber bubble, and Grace drove it swiftly over a country meadow, on wheels of air. After twenty minutes, we approached a small town and toured the main street. It was a gloomy little burg, *improved* with dozens of low-rise buildings, each a faded pastel color, but all were well maintained, other than the paint. I saw only a handful of beings in our travels, all of which seemed to be wearing the oddest of headgear and all of which seemed to be in a hurry to get from one side of the street to the other. There were no vehicles of any nature, at least, not to my eye.

"Can we get out for a bit?" I asked.

"No," Grace replied, "the air quality is hardly perfect, and if you are a man who has any allergies, you would pay the price. Those that venture outside on Desol 8 do so for only the briefest time and only with breathing apparatus—and only when they must."

"How do they travel great distances, I mean, if they need to?"

"They don't, usually, everything is nearby, their places of employment, food, medical care, entertainment, everything. When they absolutely must travel a long distance, they travel in vehicles like this, and they pay to hire them. And, it is not cheap."

"Are there a lot of towns like this one?" I inquired.

"Many, many, but not as many as there used to be."

"Animal life?" I asked.

"No, sir, not here, as with most every inhabited planet, everywhere, there is but one species on Desol 8."

...

We arrived at Heron Cove, as the day ebbed into the night. We dined at a dark, little restaurant with tiny booths. The only thing positive about the eatery was its bay view. Unfortunately, one could only enjoy that from the outside of the building. As for the food, I found it quite passable, that is, until Grace told me that it was synthetic. I then developed a retroactive dislike for the casserole and rolls and the wine.

"Synthetic food is good for you," promised Grace, "it has just the right amount of fat, protein, sugar, and vitamins. And, I think it is tasty."

"You mean synthetic fat and synthetic taste," I countered.

"True, but one's body benefits from such a diet. The people of Desol 8, on average, live very long and healthy lives."

...

The gleaming edifice rose from the landscape and into the sky as if it had equal disdain for both. Grace and I toured the new casino at Heron Cove and the resort hotel, which boasted 6,000 suites. We padded along the thick green carpet in one of the slot parlors.

"This resort will be the diamond of Desol 8," said my guide, "and it will put us on the intergalactic map, so to speak."

"When will you be up and running?" I asked.

"Not long. We will begin pre-pre-booking in about three months, while the finishing touches are completed."

I passed a row of slot machines, imagining how they might look when powered up.

"Entertainment?" I asked.

"Only the best," Grace answered, "and from every corner of the galaxy."

"I am trying to imagine what the corner of a galaxy might look like," I said.

"Don't think about it too long," Grace replied, "it will give you a headache. I am glad you came here, Mr. Quest, and I am glad you will write a story about Desol 8 and our new resort. It is very important that we get the word out. Our economy is not what is used to be."

"The resort is spectacular," I told her, "and the indoor waterfall is a nice touch, if not particularly unique. I promise that my story will reflect the majesty of the your development."

"Wonderful," she said, "anything else I can show you before we head back to home base?"

"No, but I do have a comment about the name of your planet, *Desol 8*. I understand that it is a purely unintentional, if unfortunate, play on words, but I hardly believe it will be great for your business, if you'll forgive me offering my opinion."

"I understand that," said Grace, "better than anybody. But, there is not much we can do. This planet was saved, you might say, by a brilliant entrepreneur, by the name of Albert Desol, two centuries ago. He created a business model unlike any other, and it brought great wealth to our land and its people. Of course, there were the losses of some natural resources along the way, but that was to be expected. One can't make an omelet—and so on. Anyway, our planet was named after our savior, Mr. Desol, and each time we reinvent ourselves, we add a number. Three years ago, we were Desol 7; today, we are Desol 8, in fifty years we might very well be Desol 9.

"And before Albert Desol," I asked, "what was your planet called then?"

"It was called Earth, Mr. Quest, it was called Earth. But let's just say that that was an experiment that simply did not pan out."

###

About the Author

Edward Palumbo is a graduate of the University of Rhode Island. His fiction, poems, shorts, and journalism have appeared in numerous periodicals, journals, e-journals, and anthologies, including *Rough Places Plain, Flush Fiction, Tertulia Magazine, Epiphany, The Poet's Page, Reader's Digest, Baseball Bard,* and *Dark Matter.* Ed is a prize-winning poet and playwright. His literary credo is: If you fall off the horse, get right back on the bicycle.

*****~~~~*****

Telling the Bees

by Judith Field

Mark opened the secret desk drawer and took out the ash wood wand. The warmth from the power stored in it spread through his fingers, and he felt the wood throb like a heartbeat. He muttered an incantation, and the wand folded into two. He put it into his pocket.

Pat was in the garden. He joined her, tucking his hands deep into his pockets against the chill. "We've had a call-out," he said. "Cuddly toys manifesting in a house in Burnham."

"Give me a moment, I've got to finish this. I want these carrots to set seed for next year." Looking up at the sky, she sang a golden melody about honeysuckle and summer. The wind eased. He heard his own voice singing the chorus. The buzzing of bees filled the space. One circled his head three times before landing on his hand.

"That was its way of kissing you," Pat said. "But I'm not jealous. Bees are the world's little musicians. They love singing, and it's quicker to bribe them into the veg garden with a few verses than to grow extra flowers." She shivered. "What happened to the summer?"

"Gone." He put his arm round her and looked up at the trees, almost bare of leaves. "And where are the swallows?"

"Somewhere warm, if they've got any sense. I'm glad this job's indoors." She bent over the carrot plants.

"Bye now, little musicians. Go off and do your magic. I've got to go to work. And so should you." She stood up. "You've got to keep the bees up to date with everything that's going on; they easily take offence."

They returned to the house. "Animated toys," she said. "That's usually down to life force spilling over from other duality. We need to shove it back and fix the leak. Got your wand?

He nodded, and patted his jacket pocket.

"Good. Look after it. There'll be no more. Ash dieback's put paid to that."

...

The house was on a new estate; a maze of streets built between the river and the remains of Wodehouse Forest, and leading nowhere. Pat and Mark picked their way along a muddy path flanked on either side by a row of terraced houses of different sizes, like a mouthful of broken teeth. Each had a plot number, apparently generated at random like the lottery.

On their second pass along the street, Mark spotted Plot 16, between Plots 73 and 2. Pat knocked on the door. A man, looking about thirty, answered.

"Court and Anderson? Thank God. Come in—I'm Gerry Finch."

They stepped inside. The aromatic smell of new carpets caught in Mark's throat. Two pencil drawings hung in the hall, "Josh, Reception Class," written on each. The first one showed a beast resembling a wingless dragon, wearing a top hat and a cloak. A single black eye gazed from the middle of a face that had no mouth or nose. The second showed a cross between a dog and a rabbit, with a rat-like tail and six limbs. Its mouth, looking too large for its face, was filled with long, pointed teeth.

"Josh loves to draw," Gerry said. "Teacher reckons he's got more imagination than the rest of the class put together."

He ushered them into a room at the end of the hallway. "Have a seat." Mark sat on a Chesterfield sofa covered in dazzling orange leather. Gerry perched, crossing and uncrossing his legs, on the edge of a matching, eye-watering armchair.

Pat sat beside Mark. "Gerry?"

"This is going to sound mad—"

"Not to us," Pat said. "We're used to this. Lots of entities look like toys."

"We'll try to find a way to sort it out," Mark said. Pat nudged him with her elbow. "I mean, we *will* sort it out. Just tell us your story."

"Moving here three months ago was meant to be a fresh start for me and Josh," Gerry said. "Our own garden, and backing onto a forest. I moved a couple of fence boards. Josh likes to run round in it." He bit at a fingernail. "It was all good, till a week ago." His voice thickened and tailed off.

"It's OK, take your time," Pat said.

Gerry cleared his throat. "Those toy things showed up in Josh's room, from nowhere. Hiding under the bed. He shuddered and a sheen of sweat appeared on his forehead. "I couldn't catch them."

"We can," Pat said.

"Hang on. Things got a whole lot worse. I heard a man's voice in Josh's bedroom late one night. Went in to tell him to turn his telly off. But it was a book."

Mark reached in his pocket and pulled out the phasmometer, a black object the size and shape of a goose egg, which detected entities. It emitted a series of staccato clicks, like dried peas dropping into a saucepan, one at a time. "A book with pictures, you press a button and it makes a sound?"

Gerry stood and paced up and down. "No, no. It was an ordinary book I got when I was a kid. *Treasure Island.* Forgot I still had it—it must be 20 years since I've looked at it. It was open on Josh's bed. He'd been drawing on the pages. The book was reading itself aloud. Stopped, when I came in."

"Can we see it?" Pat said.

Gerry shook his head. "I burnt it. Had to. It wasn't reading *Treasure Island.* It was some sort of poem, creepy weird stuff. I wasn't having Josh listen to that."

Mark leaned forward. "Can you recall the words?"

"Flowers. . . blood." He shook his head. "I can't remember."

"I can." A boy aged about four stood in the open doorway.

"Go back to your room, Josh," Gerry said.

"No, Dad. Listen." He looked into the distance. A dry, creaking voice came from his mouth.

"When daffodils begin to peer,
With heigh! the doxy over the dale,
Why, then comes in the sweet o' the year;
For the red blood reigns in the winter's pale,
And the sun shall flee from me in fear,
While I shall kill—"

Gerry grabbed his arm. "Shut it. That's enough."

Josh looked at his father. "I didn't say nothing."

The clicks from the phasmometer changed from single peas to a harvest. Mark showed it to Pat. "Ever seen a count rate like this?"

Her eyes opened wide. "Some massive, unstable source of power is near, and coming closer. Getting stronger." She stood. "I don't think it was Josh saying that."

Gerry let go of Josh's arm and slumped onto the sofa "What are you on about? We all saw him." He held his head in his hands. "This is doing my nut in. Just go, Josh."

Josh ran from the room. His footsteps thudded along the hallway. A door slammed.

"We need to talk to him," Pat said.

…

Pat sat next to Josh on the bed, his chin resting on the drawing pad he clutched to his chest.

Mark heard a scuffling sound.

"Look out," Josh said, curling his legs under himself, as the dog-rabbit from the drawing in the hall shot its head out from under the bed frame, nipped Pat on the ankle, and pulled its head back. "Too slow."

"Ouch!" Pat said. "See if you can flush them out, Mark. Then we'll zap them."

Mark crouched by the bed and poked underneath it with his ash wand. He felt something roll away from him and edged his hand into the gap. The tips of his fingers chilled as they closed round the object.

Pat put her arm round Josh. "It's not a very nice toy, is it?"

His face reddened, and his lower lip wobbled. "The other one's mean too. They won't let me sleep. Dad's cross all the time. It's my fault."

Pat's voice softened "Of course it's not. But, where'd they come from?"

"They just come. When I draw with Woodface's pencil."

Pat reached out for the drawing book. "Can I see?"

Josh handed it to her. She flicked through the pages, all blank.

"Can't draw any more. Lost my pencil," Josh said.

Mark stood up, holding what he had found under the bed. It looked like a bundle of twigs held together with a pencil lead in the centre. He felt the throb of a pulse deep inside it.

"Mine," Josh shouted. "Not yours. Gimme!"

Pat recoiled. "That reeks of dark magic. We need to take it away with us. Start a binding ritual to immobilise it, Mark." She turned to Josh. "Who's Woodface—your teacher? Where did he get it?"

53

"Woodface lives in the forest. I didn't steal it. I found it lying by our fence. He said I could have it."

The pencil writhed like a snake, driving a splinter into Mark's palm. He jerked his hand, and the pencil fell to the floor. Josh grabbed it and ran.

They dashed after him, into the kitchen. Gerry looked up from his seat at the table.

"He's in the garden."

Through the kitchen window Mark caught a glimpse of Josh stepping through the gap in the fence, into Wodehouse forest. He flung the back door open, and they rushed out. Turning sideways, Mark followed Josh through the gap, pulling Pat after himself.

"Wait, I'm coming too," Gerry called. He rushed at the fence and stretched out a hand towards it. With a crack, a massive spark jumped across the gap. Gerry jerked his hand back. The smell of singed hair tickled Mark's nostrils. He pulled out his wand and used it to draw the shape of a door in the gap between the panels.

Gerry extended one of his feet. He wrenched it back again. "I can't get through. What is it—electric?"

"Worse than that. No time to explain," Pat said. "You'll have to stay here. We'll find Josh."

...

Pat gripped Mark's hand. A muddy path wound between the trees, through a dense carpet of dull green leaves with saw-like edges. Mark called Josh's name. No reply. Nettles towered over them on both sides. Damp air seemed to cling to the stalks. Ragged leaves hung down, patched with white, as though splattered with dirty water.

Mark remembered a legend in a grimoire of Pat's. A tale of things in the woods, which blended among the trees without being seen. That you could hear muttering in the breeze, whispering to each other.

They reached a clearing, dotted with builders' rubble. In each corner stood an ash tree, bark flaking. The few remaining leaves were withered and blotched with black. Between the trees a blue-green net of power flickered on and off like a faulty lamp.

"Someone planted those trees," Pat said, "so that the pattern in the lines of force coming from them would keep something trapped inside. But the trees are dying, and the power's failing. Something hideous has broken free."

On the far side of the clearing stood the remains of a stone archway. As they drew closer, Mark saw that the stones that had formed its sides were carved with images of smiling, winged women with six arms, flanked by flowers. Below the waist, their insect-like bodies tapered to pointed tails.

"Nobody's done anything like this for hundreds of years," Pat said, "But it used to be standard practice to lock evil into the keystone, the centre of an arch, with carved goddesses standing guard."

"It might have stood there forever. Nobody would have known, if the builders hadn't cleared the space," Mark said.

Pat nodded. "The ash trees, now they're something I've only read about. They'd be a back up, in case the arch fell. A back up that failed. And Josh found his way in. Over there."

Josh sat on one of the fallen stones, drawing. They crept towards him. He looked up.

"I've nearly finished copying this picture of Woodface. He's there, on the ground." He pointed at the larger, wedge-shaped keystone, carved with stylised leaves, smoothed by time.

Mark looked at Josh's drawing of the leaves. At first as blurred as the ones on the stone, they grew sharper, shimmered, and regrouped into a face. The face of a man, with hair and beard made of leaves. Shoots grew out of the nostrils and open mouth.

"That's his head," Josh said. "I'm just finishing his body." The pencil scudded across the page, drawing something tall and broad, with legs like tree trunks. "All done!"

The air filled with the sound of whispering. Ivy growing on a tree rippled and turned, but there was no wind. A fern frond broke from its root with a sharp snap and writhed towards the edge of the clearing. Mark's pulse and breathing quickened. He pulled Josh to his feet. The pencil and book fell to the ground. A shape, man-like but rough-carved from lumps of wood, lumbered into the clearing, crackling as it came. It stopped an arm's length from them, its leaf-face scabbed with fungus.

"Not Woodface. Woodwose," Pat gasped. "Wodehouse. Woodwose. I should have known—this place breathes evil."

Mark pulled his wand out and jabbed it forward. He flung it away as it burst into flames, burning to fine powder.

The woodwose opened its mouth in a grin, showing teeth made of jagged stumps of rotting wood. "Ash to ashes," it said, in a voice like twigs scraping across stone. "Fetters of stone and ash can no longer hold me." It raised an arm and pointed a hand knotted like a bundle of dried roots at Mark. "Be a tree."

Mark's limbs stiffened and locked. He felt a thrill like an electric shock running up from the earth as it rose around his feet. "Pa-at," His voice was slow and mechanical, like an old-fashioned vinyl record played at the wrong speed "Bind-ing. . . "

Pat began reciting the ritual.

The woodwose raised a club-like arm and staggered towards her. Her voice faded. "Your words have no hold over me," it said. "My power is empathic. It thrives on feelings. On the fear of woman and man." It pushed her to the ground. Her ankle bent underneath her as she fell. It moved towards Josh.

With unfocussed eyes, Josh took a pace forward.

Mark tried to cry out. His jaw locked, choking the sound into a murmur.

The woodwose turned and smashed its arm into Mark's face. "Silence. A tree has no voice."

Blood dripped from Mark's nose. Clear, like sap. The woodwose turned towards Josh. "I have consumed summer. Earth will know it no more. The child awoke me. I thirst for his essence. Come."

Tree root fingers clutched Josh around the throat. His knees buckled, and he collapsed to the ground, eyes closed. A shimmering mist snaked out of his nostrils and mouth. The woodwose bent over him.

"You can't have him!" Pat dragged herself across the ground and clutched Josh's hand.

"I will devour you too, woman. But first, the boy. Younger. Sweeter." It bent lower, burying its face in the mist.

Pat dropped Josh's hand and hauled herself to her knees, gasping as she picked up one of the fallen stones from the arch. Her arms shook as she lifted it, and her fingers opened. It fell into a patch of mud, the winged goddess carved on it smiling up at the sky. Wings. Body like an insect. Mark willed his lips to open. He forced out a croak. "Tell. . . the bees."

Pat scooped up the ash from the burnt wand and held it in her cupped hands. She hobbled to her feet. "Wodewose. Hear me." The echo of her voice cracked around the clearing. The wodewose looked up. "Your empathic magic cares about feelings. But I use literal magic. And that cares about what you do." She flung the ash into its face. It howled, holding its head in its hands.

Pat turned her face to the sky and sang, "Honey bees, honey bees, hear what I say. An evil has taken the sun away. And now I beg you freely stay. And gather honey for many a day. Bonny bees, bonny bees, save us this day." She stared upwards. The woodwose lurched towards her.

Mark felt a stirring strength in the empty sky. A swirling, buzzing shadow appeared above them. The sound grew, as the swirl solidified into bees. More and more came, until the air was filled with the sound. The swarm covered the woodwose. It howled and keened as it hobbled in circles, beating at the bees with gnarled fists.

The buzzing grew louder. Mark heard noise inside his head, whining at a higher and higher pitch until his eyes watered and his ears rang. With a bang, like a car backfiring, the woodwose exploded into a mass of swirling dead leaves. Mark felt the stiffness in his muscles dissolve. He lifted a hand and rubbed his eyes.

Josh lay, surrounded by dead and dying bees, the mist gone from his face. Pat knelt by his side. "It's over, Josh. You're OK." No movement came. Pat touched his forehead. "He's cold. So cold."

With a cry, Gerry burst into the clearing. "What happened?" He pulled Pat away. He laid his head on Josh's chest. "What's wrong with him? Wake up, lad."

"I'm sorry. We were too late," Pat said.

"For what?" Gerry stood up, his lips curled into a snarl. "You and your mumbo jumbo. What have you done?"

Mark dragged his feet out of the earth that had engulfed them. He staggered towards Josh, singing the last line of the incantation. All he knew would have to be enough. ". . . save us this day."

The clouds parted, letting through a faint beam of sunlight. A bee rose from among its dead sisters. It flew towards Josh. Gerry went to swat it away. Mark grabbed his hand. "Let it come." The bee flew in a shaky circle around Josh's head three times, before landing on his nose. Josh sneezed. He opened his eyes.

About the Author

Judith Field was born in Liverpool, England, and lives in London. She is the daughter of writers, and learned how to agonize over fiction submissions at her mother's (and father's) knee. She has two daughters, a son, a granddaughter, and a grandson. Her fiction, mainly speculative, has appeared in a variety of publications in the USA and UK.

*****~~~~~*****

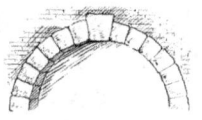

Daman

by Zerrin Otgur

Daman sat in his kitchen eating his frugal supper to the murderous bedlam of shouts and blows coming from the window: the fractious, leaderless townspeople of Tangalle were brawling in the streets again. These days the town councils and village committees of Sri Lanka only met to exchange machete whacks and insults, which they continued after hours with reinforcements in the streets. Daman's hands shook as he broke his bread. He found it hard to swallow. Out there, he knew, only the good was dying—only the humanity that was trapped deep inside even the most bloodthirsty man and woman. He had seen that good laid bare in the vacant faces of the dead who lined the streets. The good was the only thing that ever perished in this never-ending conflict, for certainly the evil survived. The evil only went from strength to strength.

Lost in such thoughts, Daman rose from his table, rinsed his loaf in the sink, put his bowl in the breadbox and his dripping loaf on the dish rack, and sank into bed, hoping never to wake again to a world in such chaos. But only an hour later, he snapped awake again, breathing hard. His lips stretched into an elated grin as he remembered the events of his vivid dream. In the dream, a king, as in the old days, ruled over them once more. "A savior of humanity!" he whispered breathlessly. In another moment he was up, dressed, and in the streets himself.

The winding alleys of Tangalle were still choked with frenzied men grappling in pools of blood, but as soon as they saw Daman, the Prophet of Tangalle, coming through the streets, they lowered their weapons, let go their opponents, and fell in behind him in a mute, orderly file: the Prophet of Tangalle was the only man they all revered alike. He was their oracle of truth and always had been. His dreams were never wrong. But it was a long time since he had had a dream, a long time since he had come out among them. In the sacred silence of this superstitious truce, they flocked behind him to the moonlit marketplace. There they waited in respectful ranks as he climbed the steps of the rough-hewed temple—the pulpit for all his prophecies. He reappeared high above in the stone bell cote and pulled the rope of the great bronze bell. As the tolls died out he looked down from the parapet and raised his voice:

"Townsfolk of Tangalle!" he cried. "One of you has had a son tonight!"

A loud grunt of surprise issued up from the back of the crowd. A weather-beaten man in a grubby white T-shirt raised his hand. "My wife's just had a little boy—Misri," he called up. Cries of wonder rippled through the congregation.

High up in the cagelike bell cote, Daman hesitated in confusion. He knew Manik all too well as one of Tangalle's most prominent troublemakers; indeed, he was instrumental in keeping up the conflict. But the dream rushed back to Daman in all its glory, and again he knew no doubt.

"Manik!" he cried. "Your boy is destined to grow up to unite us all in blessed peace at last! He will be the savior of humanity—of that good in all of you!"

This news was met with stunned silence, then came resounding cheers. Daman rejoined the crowd to joyful claps and whistles, and big Manik swept him up on his shoulders and paraded him about the square—for no people ever loathed their own bloodthirstiness as did the townspeople of Tangalle, nor worried more about that good in them that they had never seen, that only the Prophet of Tangalle could see, and for which they cherished him beyond his gift of dreams.

"Well!" said Manik setting Daman down beside the steps again, out of breath and beaming. "*My* boy, eh? Well! I sure could never have dreamed *that* up myself! And I'm glad you dreamed it—otherwise who could ever believe it?"

Daman smiled his secret smile. His pale gray eyes flashed—those famous eyes that seemed to see the past, the present, and the future all at once. "I have dreamed it," he said softly, "and it will be so."

And so it was that the townspeople of Tangalle trooped off that very morning to the western edge of the town, and there set to work painting, polishing, plastering, and upholstering the long-disused palace of Tangalle's last king, just as they had done in Daman's dream.

And lo, just as they had done in Daman's dream, the palace gardens bloomed and sang once more, the great assembly rooms gleamed and glittered, and Misri—a dream of a boy with dimpled cheeks and glossy curls, dressed in the dreamed-up costume of a snow-white tunic with gold trimming and matching gilt sandals—paced the palace halls beside his live-in mentor—none other than Daman himself.

But there, alas, discrepancies crept in. When Daman began the moral lessons so vital to his pupil's destiny—to the dream of him—Misri's howls of protest threatened to bring the palace walls back down, his shrieks to crack the panes. He wanted instead to trap little flies with grains of sugar or persecute ants, red and black, with water on the boil; and at this he excelled and progressed in no time to servants and whips. By the time he reached eighteen, the pinnacle of his sainthood in Daman's dream, he had graduated to a custom-built, historically accurate, medieval torture chamber: a full-blooded nightmare of his own that, unlike his mentor's, played out perfectly in reality down to its iron thumbscrews. It was clear to Daman then that Misri had fulfilled that alternative destiny of a preordained ruler—and become a tyrant, uniting his subjects as never before, it was true, but in fear, putting a stop to their internecine killings with tortures worse than death.

In this strange deviation from a dream, Daman stood at his post in the banquet hall, waiting on the savior of humanity slumped on sumptuous silk cushions, his fists full of sugared figs, his swollen lips lolling on the rim of his wine jug—to avoid commutes between sips—his feet tap-tapping to a catch of fiddlers scraping for a prize of life, his glazed eyes winking, blinking through a galaxy of dancing girls in enforced prance around him.

Two great tears rolled down Daman's cheeks, for the boy he had believed in while his life still lay untouched before him, and the dream of him was everything. Only another dream could explain this, he knew, but he was an old man now. He no longer dreamed of prophecies. He spent his nights profitlessly reminiscing about what might have been in a past that never was. His mind swam, and with a dreamlike horror, he heard himself blurt out:

"Misri, you're nothing but a cuckoo in both senses—parasite and lunatic! You're not the savior of anything but a host of vices!"

The fiddlers ceased in terror. The dancers paused with gasps. Misri raised his drunken, wandering eyes. He stared at his half-remembered mentor, and slowly indignation filtered through to him and bestirred his rage. He rose unsteadily, scattering cocktail cups and concubines. He came at Daman, slipping and sliding on velvet and brocade, sending up a great cloud of rose petals, and caught him neatly by the throat—for to move from one's post held a penalty of certain death.

Daman

"I am the dream and the dream is never wrong!" Misri bellowed into Daman's face.

"My dreams were never wrong before *you* came along!" piped Daman. He could not seem to help himself.

As Misri dragged Daman backwards from the room, the tyrant's recreation den danced through his skull, with its crocodile shears and Spanish ticklers, its lead sprinklers and breast rippers, its scavenger's daughter and Misri himself, skidding and squelching mad with glee on flagstones red with gore. And Daman wondered bitterly what excruciating torture would now put an end to all he had suffered in the name of his dream. That grim chamber loomed ahead, but it swept by, and dropped behind, and still the madman dragged him, staggering out to the palace portico, and plunging down the palace steps and through the palace gates into the night.

That morning the townspeople of Tangalle woke to the summoning tolls of the sacred bell, which had been silent since the night of Daman's dream, eighteen years ago. They made their way, bleary-eyed in the monsoon rain, through the streets to the marketplace. There they were appalled to see up in the belfry their precious prophet swinging by his ankles from the bell rope, weakly tolling out his struggles on the ancient bell—a humiliation worse than torture for the venerable old man. On the temple's bottom step, slumped against the archway, his cheek resting against the rough-hewed wall, slumbered the tyrant, snoring gently. Misri had, of course, remembered to slink back to the palace after he had done his cruel work—but only in his drunken dreams. The townspeople of Tangalle during all this time had still believed in their prophet's prophecy, though it had never been fulfilled. Now they began to doubt. Old Manik had lost an ear and two fingers to Misri's torture chamber, but he was one of the few who had retained his tongue. When they had taken Daman safely down from the belfry, Manik told him what everyone there was thinking: "Misri *can't* be our savior of humanity because all the humanity we have ever known has come from you—and he has almost killed you."

Daman's ears were ringing, his head throbbing, his ankles aching. "I know," he admitted miserably, rubbing his legs. "My dream was wrong."

Manik crept up to the snoring Misri and took a hard look at him. "He can't even be a son of mine," he muttered. "Bloodthirsty my son may have been, but with a sense of shame at least."

One by one, the townsfolk all stepped closer. It was only the dream through all these years that had kept Misri safe. The dream had been his palace locks, the dream had been his royal guard. Now the tyrant woke to find himself pummeled by a hail of fists and boots—to his utter astonishment, it must be said, for no tyrant can become one without support. And through this blur of kicks and blows, Misri saw his old mentor, as if in a dream, looking on with an intensity of hate and satisfaction surprising in a wise man.

"Mercy!" Misri yelped. He pointed to Daman. "It was *his* dream that made me what I am!"

"We have our own dream now," growled Manik pinning the tyrant down with his knees. "It's *this* dream of rising up and splashing in a tyrant's blood!" He drew a poniard out of his breast pocket—a memento filched during his sojourn in this tyrant's nightmare—and held it up to Daman. "Put an end to your dream for us at last," he said.

Daman snatched the blade; eagerly he bent over the tyrant, but at a glance he could see—oh yes, he saw—the tyrant was gone. All that was left of him was a blubbering, bleeding coward with eyes wide with terror, begging only for his life, which was his, after all. Daman let the dagger slip from his fingers. "You can never kill a tyrant," he muttered, "just a man, only a man. Evil is a survivor, and it has gone—into you now, into me."

Daman

"The tyrant will be back before we know it if we let him go," said Manik.

"Perhaps," said Daman, "but it is only the coward of this moment that I can kill."

"*Someone* has to answer for what Misri's done!" cried Manik.

"Then let this man answer," said Daman. "Put him behind bars on bread and water. Give him hours of hard labor—a regimen a tyrant will be unlikely to return to—but spare his life for me."

Manik's expression wavered between irritation and admiration. Suddenly a look of complete comprehension flashed into his face. "Wait a minute," he said. He glanced round at the others. All of them were now staring at Daman with expressions of dawning realization. "It is *Daman* who is our savior of humanity!" cried Manik. "He always was—it just took my boy to make us realize! His dream was *true!*"

With whoops and cheers, they lifted Daman onto their shoulders, carried him back to the palace, and set him on the throne; and so at last the prophet saw his dream come true—in the manner of oracles.

About the Author

Zerrin Otgur is the author of "A Patron for a Painter," and "The Moneyed Pilgrim," among other stories. Her work has appeared in *Chapman* and *Page & Spine*. She currently resides in Boston.

*****~~~~~*****

You Can Not Have a Meaningful Campaign If Strict Time Records Are Not Kept

by Desmond Warzel

The Commonwealth of Worlds had seen better days. Its final conquest by the Galactic Hegemony was imminent, with only a handful of planets remaining free.

Commonwealth vessels were being launched and destroyed so quickly that the commissioning body was running out of names and was often forced to improvise. Infantry landing ships, for instance, were traditionally named after famous enlisted men. The approved historical figures were long-exhausted, and the criteria had been modified.

So it was that the *CWS Maxwell Q. Klinger* set down on a nondescript, uninhabited planet well outside the main theaters of combat. Symbolically, it carried within it the hopes of an entire galaxy desperate to throw off the yoke of Hegemony oppression. More tangibly, it carried ten very uncomfortable men, for the *Klinger* (more of a pod than a true ship) was designed for only six. Its sister vessel, the *CWS Gomer Pyle*, had suffered catastrophic engine success (in the sense that both engines had engaged properly, but in opposite directions), so Major Wise's squad had made the best of things.

69

The planet had sparse vegetation and even sparser animal life. It was riven with crevasses and box canyons that led nowhere. Major Wise and his aide, Lieutenant Kurosawa, stood on a precipice overlooking the terminus of one such canyon, which extended several kilometers before widening into a roughly circular depression.

Four of the men fanned out into their assigned positions; the remaining four piloted the *Klinger* farther along the canyon in order to assume their own posts.

The planet was nominally controlled by the Hegemony, but as it no longer held strategic importance, the only sign of its "occupation" was a small stone obelisk (upon which Major Wise had very nearly impaled the *Klinger*).

Lieutenant Kurosawa read aloud from the marker. "May 4, 2368: Here brave men and women of the Galactic Hegemony captured the Joint Commanders of the savage forces of the Commonwealth of Worlds, turning the tide of the Great War and saving humankind from eternal tyranny."

"'Captured!'" spat Wise. "Like a lion 'captures' a zebra, they were captured."

"What's a zebra?" asked Kurosawa.

Wise ignored the question. He passed Kurosawa a laminated sheet. "Were you briefed?"

"I just got the call an hour ago." Kurosawa was in for Wyler, whose final service to the Commonwealth had been testing the engines on the *Pyle*.

"About ten years ago, our Joint Commanders were holed up in an underground safe-house right beneath our feet. The Hegemony got wind, so the Commanders tried to flee. Their escape vessel was in that circular hollow at the other end of the canyon. They never had a chance. The Hegemony fried everything electronic with a localized EMP, then swooped in and crushed them during the confusion. See those mounds of rubble? The

Commanders, their staff, and their entire armored caravan are entombed under there."

"'03:55, ground transportation commences; light rainfall,'" Kurosawa read. "'04:00, electromagnetic pulse; all systems disabled. 04:08, torrential rain commences, visibility compromised.' What is this? Paper?"

"That's the only record of the battle from our side. It just surfaced. Handwritten by a Sergeant LeRoy, known for carrying a pen, a notebook, and a pocket watch into battle. Along with a serious taste for the old-fashioned, apparently."

"What's a pocket watch?" mused Kurosawa.

"This is a precision operation. Everyone's time device is slaved to mine; we depart simultaneously and arrive in the past at appropriately spaced intervals to maintain surprise and secure maximum advantage."

"You don't trust your own handpicked men not to desert?"

"I've no idea of their bravery or cowardice. I selected them for their names."

'Whimsical, to be sure, Major, but also frivolous, don't you think?"

"How so?"

"Aronofsky, Bakshi, Carpenter, Dante; these are all historical directors of films."

"What's a film?" muttered Wise. "Lieutenant, the positions on my map have alphabetical designations: A, B, C, and so on. How else am I to remember which man goes where without constantly referring to a key?"

This was a logic Kurosawa was ill-armed to combat.

"Huston has a duplicate of my master time device, just in case," the Major continued. "Him, I trust. His reputation precedes him."

"This Huston is an exemplary soldier?"

"He has no choice. Half his extended family fights for the Hegemony. If he ever slacked off, we'd probably hang him for a spy. Okay, everyone's in position. You and I will emerge at 04:05; that's after the EMP but before the heavy rain starts. We'll have a few minutes to look over the terrain."

...

When Wise and Kurosawa emerged ten years prior, the wind and rain, in combination with the muddy ground, caught them off guard, and they ended up on their backs.

"This is light rain?" Kurosawa scrambled and nearly achieved uprightness, but his feet had other plans and shot out from under him once more. "Where did this Sergeant LeRoy grow up, underwater?"

Wise calmly sat up, ignoring the cold water seeping through his fatigues, and studied the canyon through a pair of binoculars. Along the bottom, the caravan of armored crawlers carrying the Joint Commanders moved slowly and steadily over the rocky terrain toward the escape ship.

"Looks like a line of ants all headed for the same piece of fried chicken."

"What's a chicken?" Kurosawa asked absently as he finally got to his feet.

"That's not right, though. Why are they still moving? It's 04:07; the EMP went off seven minutes ago."

"Perhaps someone already came back and prevented it."

"It would have been nice of them to tell us," said the Major. "If I find out who's responsible, there won't be an epoch remote enough for them to hide in."

Kurosawa glanced up at the sky. "I wouldn't worry about that."

There was a momentary disturbance in the cloud cover. Wise and Kurosawa watched the object, small but unmistakably a missile, shoot straight toward the canyon and impact on the bottom directly in front of the caravan.

There was no explosion worthy of the name; merely a wave expanding outward in all directions, detectable mainly by the way it perturbed the rainfall.

They felt nothing as the wave passed through them. In the canyon, the crawlers ground to a halt. Their motors still hummed, but the computers that controlled their hydraulics were now inert.

"That's not right," repeated Wise. "Damn that sergeant and his stupid pocket watch. All my tech is shot. Yours?"

"Just a bunch of expensive doorstops and Christmas tree ornaments at this point."

"What's a Christmas tree?"

"What do we do now, Major?"

"Hold tight, wait for the others, deal with the situation as it develops. It could be worse; Wyler could be here."

"The man I replaced? What if he were?"

"*He* had a pacemaker." Major Wise indicated the laminated sheet, which Kurosawa still clutched. "What's next on Sergeant LeRoy's agenda?"

"'04:17, approx. five hovertanks attack from western branch canyon, crawlers now permanently disabled, numerous casualties.'"

"What time is it now?"

"No idea. Perhaps you recall the electromagnetic pulse of several minutes ago?"

"I've got four men arriving right at 04:17 to take out those tanks: Aronofsky and Bakshi on the near side of the branch canyon, Carpenter and Dante on the far side."

"'04:19,'" Kurosawa continued. "'Some personnel attempting escape via hull breaches; all-terrain troop carriers arrive from nearmost eastern branch canyon, initiate barrage of rocket-propelled grenades; avalanches from both sides, escapees killed, remainder, including myself, surely trapped for good.'"

73

"Eastwood, Fellini, and Guy are scheduled to handle that."

"'04:21, troop carrier emerges from farmost eastern branch canyon, approaches escape vessel (surely already neutralized by EMP?); engineers rig vessel for demolition and detonate; all hope for escape gone.'"

"Huston's set to pick off those engineers from the rim of that depression."

"'Know that my allegiance remained true until the end. LeRoy, signing off.'"

Both Wise and Kurosawa found themselves compelled to kneel; not because of the solemnity of LeRoy's closing sentiment, but because the sergeant's promised deluge suddenly made itself known. The rain no longer fell in drops, but in great discrete masses of water that lashed at the two men's backs and gouged furrows in the bare soil.

"I guess it's 04:08," Kurosawa remarked dryly (to the extent that he could do *anything* dryly).

"But it *isn't*," muttered Wise. "Even if LeRoy thinks it is. He's down there right now, you know. I have half a mind to go haul him out of that crawler myself. Why should the Hegemony have the pleasure of killing him?"

Ahead and to the left, barely visible through the rain, were four brief flashes of light.

"That will be A, B, C, and D," said Kurosawa. "That makes it 04:17, I guess. But I don't hear any hovertanks."

There came several seconds of light and noise, after which the sound of tumbling rocks and subsiding earth was evident even over the sound of the rain.

"Did what I think happened, just happen?" asked the Major.

"What?" asked Kurosawa. "That Aronofsky, Bakshi, Carpenter, and Dante, upon emerging here in the past, were disoriented by the heavy rain and unable to confirm the presence of the hovertanks due to the low visibility, and so decided to assume the accuracy of the orders you gave and open fire with their rocket launchers, which in the absence of said hovertanks merely undermined the canyon walls, causing the entire thing to collapse and take them with it? Is that what you think happened?"

"Well, I wouldn't have been so verbose about it."

There were three flashes, ahead and to the right this time.

"That'll be Eastwood, Fellini, and Guy," observed Kurosawa.

There was a further disturbance of light and noise as the arrivals fired on the position they assumed the Hegemony's troop carriers to occupy, and, once more, the sound of settling rocks and earth.

"Come *on*," raged Major Wise impotently. "Show a little discernment, how about it?"

"Did you order them to show discernment, or to open fire on arrival?"

"You think you're being helpful, but you're not," said the Major. "I've been giving orders continuously for twenty-five years; nobody obeys them, and never twice in a row. They had to pick *today*?"

The faintest of flashes marked the arrival of Huston at the far end. There were no further disturbances at his position.

"Thank the angels for small favors—"

"What's an angel?" asked Kurosawa.

"—not that it'll do us any good if we can't communicate with him."

Approximately four minutes went by. Kurosawa knew this because he'd been mentally counting "one Mississippi, two Mississippi" since Huston's arrival, even though he had no idea what Mississippi was.

Then the attack commenced. It was almost exactly as LeRoy had documented, except that the hovertanks and troop carriers had to negotiate the extra rubble created by the time travelers' impulsive and ultimately suicidal actions. Wise and Kurosawa could only watch. Their sidearms, though functional, would have been ineffective and served only to give away their location.

The major and the lieutenant retreated out of sight of the canyon. They found no cover, but they did stumble across a slanted boulder against which they could rest upright, thereby lessening, however slightly, the ignominy of their potential deaths.

Despite the fact that they'd barely spent half an hour in the past, both men were exhausted and quickly nodded off, oblivious to the crippling precipitation flogging their unconscious bodies.

...

Wise awoke to find the rain had ceased. Several yards away, the third surviving member of their contingent stood guard, scanning the horizon.

"Huston, we have a problem," said Wise as he struggled to his feet.

Huston snapped off a salute. "The Hegemony forces have departed. Are you all right, Major?"

"Good as can be expected." He nudged the sleeping Kurosawa with his boot. "Look alive, Lieutenant. We have company."

Kurosawa rose. "You must have had some hike, Huston."

"A little rappelling, a bit of climbing. I kept my mind busy calculating how much suspicion will fall on me for the failure of this mission."

"I can't figure it, Huston. How could *every* time-stamp be off? And in such a weirdly precise way?"

"I think I've solved that, Major," said Huston. "I have many relatives living and serving under the Hegemony. We don't speak, of course, but I get a lot of info by osmosis. Did you know, for instance, that the Hegemony uses a twenty-three hour day?"

"That makes no sense," said Wise. "Each hour would be--"

"Sixty-two point six minutes," supplied Kurosawa.

"Sixty-two minutes even, sirs," said Huston.

"But then there would be—"

"Fourteen minutes left over," supplied Kurosawa.

"Right," said Wise. "What do they do, tack them on at the day's end?"

"They add them to the noon hour," said Huston. "So they can take longer lunches."

"What's the point?" Kurosawa asked.

"That's revolution for you," interjected Wise. "Change for change's sake. You overthrow one government, suddenly it's 'metric system' this and 'Thermidor' that."

"Irrespective of purpose," said Huston, "it accounts for the discrepancy. LeRoy's pocket watch was obviously of Hegemony manufacture. Whether he was actually a Hegemony agent, or he just took the watch as a war trophy, who can say?"

"Kurosawa and I came in at 04:05 Commonwealth time—after the EMP, or so we thought. What time was it by LeRoy's cockamamie watch?"

"03:59 Hegemony time."

"And the EMP?"

"It came three minutes later, at 04:00 Hegemony time, just as LeRoy noted," said Huston.

"How is 04:00 three minutes after 03:59?"

"Sixty-two minutes in an hour, sir; remember? 03:59, 03:60, 03:61, 04:00."

"I didn't think it was possible to hate the Galactic Hegemony more that I already did," said Wise.

"We should head back and report in, sirs." Huston unsnapped a belt pouch and slipped out his time device. "I believe I'm set up to do the honors for all of us."

"When you're ready," said Wise.

"I'm not looking forward to this," said Huston as he thumbed the switch.

"Huston, wait! We're not slaved to you anymore because—"

Kurosawa was cut off by the flash of Huston's departure.

"—our devices are fried," he finished lamely.

"I really thought he was sharper than that," said Wise.

"He'll be back," said Kurosawa. "Probably in a few seconds; that's the beauty of time travel."

...

"He's probably not coming," said Wise an hour later.

"I honestly don't understand it," said Kurosawa.

"Don't you? What would you do if you were a bright young man with the *CWS Maxwell Q. Klinger* at your disposal and the galaxy's only functioning time machine in your pocket? You might head to the Hegemony and reconcile with your family, or retire to some more peaceful historical era, or a dozen other things, none of which involve continuing your military career."

"The *only* time machine?"

"There *were* ten of them, until today. It's brand-new tech. Didn't you wonder why you'd never heard of time travel before today?"

"I assumed it was classified."

Wise sighed. "Well, even on a ball of mud like this, there's *something* edible. We stay alive until we can leave."

"But the next ship isn't due for ten years, and it's *us*," said Kurosawa. "Just thinking about it gives me a headache."

"Not quite true. Somebody's coming by to place that commemorative marker. We jump them, take their ship, and go straight to Commonwealth HQ to spill everything we know about the next ten years of the war."

You Can Not Have a Meaningful Campaign

"It has the feel of a terrible idea," said Kurosawa, "but for some reason I can't think of anything better."

"Did the marker's inscription include the date of placement?"

"It did."

"When was it?"

"I have no idea."

"*None?*"

"I didn't have a chance to make a rubbing before we left."

Wise had no retort. He went and sat on the nearby boulder. Kurosawa joined him.

"In future, Kurosawa, this is my side. Your side's around back. The less we look at each other, the longer until we hate each other."

"I suppose you're not wrong."

"I could really go for some vodka about now."

"What's vodka?" asked Kurosawa. "You know, it's no wonder humanity's constantly fighting with itself. No one knows anything; the culture's too fragmented."

Wise sighed and massaged his temples. "Vodka is a fish preparation popular where I grew up."

The sarcasm flew by the lieutenant without stopping. "I bet we could find some fish. All that rainwater must collect somewhere."

"Feel free, Kurosawa. I'm heading back. The ship carrying that marker might land today. I want to be underneath it if it does."

About the Author

Desmond Warzel is the author of a few dozen short stories in the science fiction, fantasy, and horror genres. These have appeared in venerable magazines like *Fantasy & Science Fiction*, in nifty anthologies like

Coven: Masterful Tales of Fantasy (Purple Sun Press), and on new-fangled podcasts like *The Drabblecast*. He lives in northwestern Pennsylvania.

*****~~~~~*****

Racial Memory

by Gustavo Bondoni

"Grandpa, can you tell me about the fairies?"

"Again? You really like the fairies, don't you? Do you want me to read you a bit of this book of fairy stories?"

"No, not those. Those are stupid. I want to know about the real fairies. You said you knew the story. You said you'd tell me where they went."

"Not where they went, but where they were last seen."

"Isn't it the same thing?"

"No, this happened a long time ago, far away from here."

"Far, like McMurray Street?"

"Much further."

"Wow. Where? Have I been there?"

"Hmm. I don't know, have you ever been to the Olduvai Gorge?"

"What? There's no such place, you're making things up…"

…

At the bottom of a deep, steep hole in Africa, a girl looked up at the night sky. She didn't know she was a girl, she didn't even know what a girl was. All she really knew was that the night sky had pretty lights in it and that there were things that were good to eat, and things that made you sick. There were also things that liked to eat things

81

like her, but there weren't all that many of them that would dare to attack a big girl with a spear. Those things and the trees and the walls of the valley made up the category she mentally called "the world." The world was half of what she thought about.

Most of the rest of what she thought about was the group. The girl didn't know what a family was, she didn't know what a clan was. She just knew that there were other things like her living in the hole—which was actually a valley, but one with walls so steep that no one had ever climbed them—and that they shared their food with her and that she had to share her food with them. In her mind, they were "people," and there were man-people and woman-people in the group.

The reason this girl had to think these things out by herself was that she lived very far back in time, in what is called prehistoric times. In fact, she lived so far back that the only people living in the world all lived in Africa. And of those people, only the most intelligent and adventurous had made it as far as the Olduvai Gorge, which does, in fact, exist, but it doesn't look like it did back then. Water and wind have softened the sides, and made it much easier to climb in and out of now than it was back then.

The girl's grandparents' grandparents had seen a lush forest that looked like it had food in it and climbed down the side, but, by the time she'd been born, there was no one left alive who knew how to get back out again. And the group had broken into other, smaller groups, which had grown, and it was dangerous to pass their territory. They would keep any girls they saw tied up until they were old enough for children. The girl didn't want children because they had to be carried, and smelled, and you had to give them food from your own body.

But right at that moment, she wasn't thinking about her people, and she wasn't thinking about the world. She was watching one of the tiny glowing creatures, about the size of her hand, that shared the valley with them. It was trapped, one wing caught between a rock and the floor, and its efforts to escape were achieving little, apart from putting a huge strain on the wing. It would tear off soon, leaving the creature—shaped like one of her people, but lighter-skinned and much, much smaller—to the mercy of the scurrying things that roamed through the underbrush.

The girl got into a more comfortable position, and sat still. She was afraid to touch the glowing creature—everyone knew that some members of her group had been touched by the glowing ones, and they had been driven mad by impossible visions and nightmares—but she was perfectly willing to let something else come along to try to victimize it. Maybe whatever came along would be edible. Maybe it would just be fun to watch.

The fairy—and that was what it was, even though the girl didn't know it—saw her and looked straight into her eyes. It stopped struggling. Were it not for that useless, pale-colored skin that would have looked better on a fish than on a person who had to walk in the sun, it would have looked exactly like an adult woman-person. It stayed still, which kept it from breaking the wing, but wouldn't help much if something hungry came along. The girl recognized that look. It was the look that trapped animals gave her just before she hit them with her spear.

But she didn't hit the fairy with her spear. She did something that surprised even herself.

The girl lifted the rock.

And the fairy. . . Well, the fairy flew away as fast as its injured wing allowed it to.

. . .

"It flew away?"

"Of course it did. What did you expect?"

"I don't know, fairy stuff. Gold. Treasure. Wishes!"

"But what would a girl like that do with gold?"

"You're right, she's like a caveman, isn't she?"

83

"Well, not exactly. They didn't live in caves there. And she was a girl, so she couldn't be a caveman at all."

"But like a caveman, or a cavegirl, or whatever."

"Yes, like one. But not exactly one."

"All right. But what about the fairies?"

"I'll tell you more about them tomorrow."

…

The girl walked through the densest forest.

Some parts of the great valley were open, grassy and ideal for hunting, because you could see a long way, but the girl tended to avoid those places. What helped you hunt food also allowed things that ate people to hunt you—and it also allowed other tribes to hunt girls like her. She preferred the safety of the dark shadows and recessed nooks.

And besides, in the shadows, she could see the soft light of the flying people. Their loops and stunts made her smile—and some of the more amazing swoops actually caused her to laugh out loud.

But the main reason she went there wasn't for safety or for entertainment. It was so that she wouldn't have to share her food with the others. She knew how to get food from the forest, and, if she were careful to wash off the blood afterward, no one would know that she'd eaten, and they'd give her a share of what the other hunters brought back with them.

Her method was simple. All she would do was to rub leaves and dirt on her body, and sit inside a bush next to one of the paths that the animals used to get to the flowing water that ran through the middle of the valley. If she stayed very still, one of the bolder animals would walk past. It was usually something a little too big to attack with her spear, but, egged on by its success, smaller forms would soon appear.

A small, furry creature walked into sight, moving slowly and raising its head to sniff the air suspiciously every two or three steps. The girl held her breath, hoping that this one wouldn't sense her and be spooked. Two or three of the glowing people flew above her head, but they were common enough that perhaps the small creature wouldn't realize that they marked her position.

It was close enough, now, to strike. But the girl waited. One more step.

All of a sudden, the creature seemed to realize its danger, looked straight at the place where the girl was hidden, and turned.

At the same moment, she threw the spear with all her strength, knowing immediately that she'd missed slightly to one side. The creature saw it coming and spooked, swerving at high speed away from the missile, and away from her. It brushed the branch of a low thorn-bush and then, with a crash, cartwheeled into the tangle of thorns. It lay there, twitching one limb or other experimentally.

The girl could see that it wouldn't go anywhere. Every time it moved, all it did was to bury the spikes impaling it a little deeper into its flesh. She watched it struggle, seeing no need to hurry, and the flying people-things gathered around her.

But this wasn't a strange and possibly dangerous glowing person. This was food, and the girl picked up her spear and, without pausing, buried it in the creature's torso. It squealed once, and then struggled, freeing itself from the thorns.

The spear, however, was too much for it, passing all the way through its body. The food was dead within moments.

She danced with the joy of capture, of feeding and of life. She pulled the creature out of the bush, still impaled on the spear, and set it down before her. She knew that if she took it to her group, most would be taken from her. Maybe the group would use its captive ember to make a fire and cook some of the meat, and that would be delicious.

But it was worth sacrificing taste to have more for herself. She used the sharpened point of the spear to puncture the hide until she could tear the creature open to get at the meat under the hair.

The flying people-things came closer. She ignored them as she let some of the blood fall onto the ground, drying the meat inside enough that she could see what she was doing. She ignored them until one, the one she had saved earlier, still flying unsteadily on its bent wing, appeared right in front of her face, between the girl and her food. It looked straight into the girl's eyes and reached out an arm. Its tiny finger touched the girl on the nose and the world exploded.

...

"That's it?"

"Go to bed now."

"But that's a terrible ending. How could the world explode? And besides, you said this was a long time ago. The world couldn't have exploded. It's still here."

"It's a metaphor, I think."

"A what?"

"It's a word that means something else. I think the story will go on tomorrow."

"Tell me the rest now!"

"I. . . I can't. I haven't heard the rest yet."

"You mean you haven't made it up yet."

"If you prefer. Now, lights off and go to bed."

...

The girl sat down hard on the grass. The trees around her came into focus slowly, and, for the first time in her life, they had names. They weren't the names that you or I know, but they had ceased to be classified simply by whether they had thorns or not, or edible fruit, or the ones that made you sick if you ate the nuts. Each was individual, similar to some, different from the rest.

Likewise, the bloody animal she'd hunted – some sort of rodent – had a name. It wasn't just a walking piece of meat, too small to defend itself. It was a type of animal. The names, and many other words, more words than her group had ever formed, more words than could possibly exist, poured into the girl's head.

"Can you hear me?"

The girl looked around. Who was there? Only her people spoke, and her own group never came into the woods. She picked up her spear, pointing it in the direction she thought the sound had come from, but otherwise stayed very, very still.

"You won't need that."

The girl reeled. Her mind wasn't having trouble with the voice, and it wasn't having trouble with what the voice was saying. It was having trouble with the fact that such a difficult concept—the negation of something that hadn't yet happened—could be conveyed with words. Words were small things. One meant "food," another meant "danger." One meant "man" and another "woman." "Come" and "go." They were for basic things. Words were so few, so precious, that there was even a word for "word." But such a complicated structure was an impossibility.

Especially since it had been expressed in words she'd never heard before. She straightened, spear at the ready.

"Really, we mean no harm."

Again, her mind retreated in the face of impossibility, but enough of her consciousness remained to attempt to find its source. The words seemed to be coming from the forest itself, a small, piping note out of the thickest branches of the trees in front of her.

"We?" she asked. Why she should know any words in that language was beyond her, but it was obvious that she did. "Who are you? Show yourselves."

Branches rustled just above her eye level, and she adjusted her stance to face them directly. A single glowing form floated out of the tree.

"It is I who speaks to you." It was a woman-shaped fairy, the same one she'd saved earlier.

The same one, she suddenly remembered, that had touched her face before.

The girl fell in a heap. "What have you done to me?"

The images of the mad folk, failing to keep their eyes focused, so useless that everyone had to share food with them while they gave none in return, speaking in gibberish and unable to understand what was said in turn. They were sad, forlorn figures.

And now she was one of them.

The girl cried, and wondered whether it would be safe to vent her anger on the shining creature floating beside her. After all, what could harm her more than madness? There was nothing left for her to give. But even without words, the rumors existed, and everyone in the group—new words like "tribe" and "family" floated through her mind, but she fought against them fiercely, knowing that they were but steps on the path of madness—was aware of the dark fate that awaited one who hurt a glowing creature. The word "fey" she also ignored. She wasn't sure what it meant, anyway, other than something much like "people."

But her new mind, actually her old mind with all the new words in it, wouldn't let her dwell on the misery that awaited her. It ate through the despair and threw it aside. One single question remained, burning like fire—not the tame fire of her village, but the hungry flame that lived in lightning. "Why have you done this to me?"

The woman-thing didn't hesitate. "Because you are different."

"I am different because you made me different. Now I will be useless to the tribe. . . to people. My food will all be shared food."

The woman-thing hovered right in front of her and met her gaze directly. "You were already different before."

...

"But why was she different? I want to know now!"

"You will go to sleep. Perhaps you'll find out more tomorrow."

"Don't you know?"

"It all depends on what I hear in the night."

"Is she a fairy?"

"Who, the girl?"

"No, the glowing woman."

"I think so. Yes, I'd say she probably is. Go to sleep now."

...

"Why did you make me crazy?" the girl asked the fairy. "I was happy." Happiness was another concept that was completely new to her, but one that immediately brought up an image of sitting on the ground near her tribe and watching the stars in the night sky.

"I didn't make you crazy. You are still the same as you were, but I just gave you the words to understand the world."

"I understood my world before you touched me."

"You might have understood your world, but you didn't understand the world. Now you do—or you will once you stop questioning what can't be undone and start thinking about things."

"Everyone else you've touched went mad."

The fairies—for the original woman-thing had been joined by two of the men-things—hovered silently for a moment.

"Yes, they all have. Opening them up to the world was too much for them; their minds broke. We swore to leave you in peace, to let you be like the animals you eat, and like the ones that eat you." She paused to look at the girl again. "But I saw that you could tell the difference between beast and thinking creature."

"You mean because I saved you?"

"Yes."

"Maybe I did it because you were pretty." The girl was amazed at the way words—nothing but words—allowed her to express thoughts she wouldn't have had otherwise.

"Did you?"

"No." The girl thought. "What was it that broke their minds?"

"It isn't always the same thing."

"Is it two things?" Counting was easier than many of the other things she'd learned, but she was still trying to get a feel for how they related to anything but her fingers.

The fairy tinkled, a sound that the girl would come to know as laughter, but not to understand.

"It is many things, but it is mainly just two."

"Tell me."

"I don't want your mind to break."

"I'll come to it myself sooner or later."

Eyes downcast, the fey replied: "Yes, you probably will."

"Tell me."

"The first thing is names. Your kind seems to have trouble understanding that people are different from other people, and that each can be called something different, not just man or woman. My name is Lenii, and that is Guoo, and that is Drioo."

"You are all fey." The word was right for them.

"Yes, but we are different fey."

The girl tried to wrap her mind around this concept. She thought she could actually feel it breaking under the strain as things gave way. If they were different things, they could act as they wanted. They could go different places and hunt different food. They. . . And suddenly the world changed again. "Can I have a name?"

The fairy smiled.

...

"How could she not have a name? People always have names."

"I think this was before people knew they were people."

"Why do you keep saying that you think this and you think that? It's your story, grandpa."

"It is? Well, no matter. Lights out."

...

"The other question," Tiam said.

"What do you mean?"

"The other question that breaks our minds."

"That one is more serious."

"You thought giving me a name might do it," Tiam reminded her fey friend.

"None of your kind has survived this."

"I think I will," the young woman who, before the gift of the fairies, had thought of herself as just another one of the people, told her friend. She was lying. In fact, her mind was already beginning to fail. Over the past few moons, her understanding of everything had grown incredibly, but at the same time, her fairy teachers had grown more and more indistinct. There were moments in which she could see straight through Lenii, and the two males had long since disappeared. One thing that all of her tribe knew was that the fey were there, had always been there, and would always be there. So not being able to see them anymore could not possibly be a good sign.

Lenii hesitated, but spoke. "It is about the walls of the valley."

"What about them? They mark the edge of the world."

"No, they don't. There is another world beyond them."

"It can't be a very big world, or we would hear it."

"It is a world much bigger than the world within these walls. It is so large it would take you many, many years to cross it all."

Tiam stood, trying to see over the cliffs. "That cannot be."

"It is."

She thought and thought. The more she thought, the more her mind rebelled against the idea. Everything her family needed was inside the walls: water, food, stones, and wood for spears. What need could the world have of anything else? She said as much to the fairy.

"I can show you the path to the top."

"Why has no one found it?"

"Because they don't believe it exists."

So, they climbed among the shrubbery, and by the time they reached the final ledge, night had fallen. Even Tiam's strong young limbs were sore by that time. But the silver light of the moon showed nothing but a long, flat expanse. "See? It's empty. Let's go back."

"If you trust me, wait for day."

So Tiam wedged herself in the crook of a tree—the only way to be safe in the night—and slept as well as she could. Her family would probably have given her up for dead by then, but they would be happy to see her when she returned. Unlike the other mad members of the tribe, she'd tried to teach them a few things at a time. They thought she was simply some kind of very young elder—and elders were to be respected and revered.

The pink beginning of day woke her. She looked toward the rising sun, but her eyes never reached the horizon. In front of her, and to every side, a great expanse of land full of trees, bushes and animals of every description extended. It went on forever, until the land ended at the horizon. It was something that, after the close walls of the valley, seemed to be a fantasy. But it was there, in front of her eyes, and her eyes would never lie to her.

"Lenii, it's beautiful!" Tears came to her, and she was overwhelmed. "It's beautiful, Lenii," she said again, after the tears had subsided.

But no answer came. Lenii was not there with her.

She climbed back down, half-sliding, but her friend was nowhere to be found. In fact, not one single fey, not one single glowing tiny creature was to be seen in the whole valley—even though it had once been impossible for Tiam to move more than a few steps without seeing one.

Her tears came in earnest now. Not the crying of one moved by beauty but that of one sobbing for a huge loss. She knew that she would never know them again, and had been left with no company but that of her fellow people, who could barely understand the glimmer of what she'd been shown.

It would take a lifetime to teach them everything. A lifetime to make them understand even a fraction of the knowledge.

But she knew she would have to try. If she didn't, she would simply descend into madness like the others.

In another immediate decision, she knew that she would lead them out of the valley. She tried to tell herself that it was because the large land outside would give them more food, and that it was because they would follow her if she told them about more food.

But the truth was that she could hear that vast emptiness calling to her, telling her that it needed people to be complete.

It called her with a force too strong to ignore.

...

"Is that how people came here?"

"It might be."

"It's not a good story if you don't know how it ends!"

"All I know is what I hear at night. There are voices that tell me the stories."

93

"Have you always heard these voices, grandpa?"

"No, only since I began to get sick. I heard them for the first time on the day the doctors said my mind was giving out."

"Do they tell you stories every night?"

"No, they only tell one story, this one. They also say they miss us."

"Who are they?"

"I don't know. I've never seen one."

"Is it the fairies?"

"Maybe."

"All you ever say is maybe."

"That's true. And maybe you'll understand that when you get older."

"Maybe?"

"I really hope you will. Now, it's time for bed."

"Good night, Grandpa."

"Goodbye, dear one."

About the Author

Gustavo Bondoni was born in Argentina, which, he believes, makes him one of the few—if not the only—Argentinian fiction writers writing primarily in English. He moved to the US at the age of three, because his father worked for a multinational company that bounced him around the world every three years

His fiction spans the range from science fiction to mainstream stories, passing through sword and sorcery and magical realism along the way, and it has been published in fourteen countries and seven languages to date. He has published three collections, a short novel, and a novella. His website is at gustavobondoni.com.

*****~~~~~*****

94

The White Picket Fence

by A. P. Sessler

The blue sky quickly turned gray, like a fading color photograph or TV going on the fritz. Still Johnny refused to walk any faster, for every fragment, every fragile bit of time with Suzy was like a precious stone.

They walked along the quiet neighborhood block, the first from the main road. They passed a series of quaint, small-town homes on their way to Suzy's house. The walk wasn't much different from dozens before. Every day they made that same walk.

From the moment they stepped off the bus, the smoldering ember of love would be fanned by the gentle wind blowing through the breezeway of houses that lined either side of the street. And each day as soon as the red glow appeared just beneath the surface—cheeks a-flush with rushing blood and hands about to gush with perspiration—the embers were dampened by the dreadful sight of the short, white picket fence.

The waist-high fence was topped with triangular spears. An unsuccessful attempt to jump or climb over it might end in an unpleasant injury, not that there was any reason to do so. It lined the yard of the house just before Suzy's, where either her mother or father would be waiting, arms crossed, fingers drumming or foot tapping until the two youngsters separated.

"We'll be to my house soon," she said in somber tone.

"I know," he said and purposely slowed his pace while gazing at the sidewalk cracks. "You think your parents will let you go to the dance Friday night?"

He paused before facing her; afraid, unwilling, to hear her answer.

"They say I'm too young to go steady," she said.

Just as he thought. "It's a dance, not a date. Everyone will be there. I don't wanna go by myself."

"Neither do I."

They shared a mutual sigh.

Johnny looked back at the cracks beneath his feet. If he stared at them, he wouldn't see the end of the fence, and they could keep walking on and on, together—but only if she did likewise.

He counted the cracks. One. . . two. . .

"We've come to the end of the picket fence," she said.

He reluctantly looked up, hopeful she was somehow mistaken.

The corner post of the fence stood to their right, and the thin strip of grass between sidewalk and fence changed height and color from the neighbor's yard to hers.

"I'll see you tomorrow," he said.

She placed a hand on top and bottom of the pile of schoolbooks in his arms and pulled them to her breast. "Thanks for carrying my books."

"It was nothing," he said, his back popping as he stood straight.

They smiled at one another until a crack of thunder interrupted.

"I better get going," she said.

"Hurry up, Susan, before the rain starts," came her mother's voice from the raised porch of the gray two-story home.

Johnny and Suzy turned to find Mrs. Brumsley holding the screen door open with one hand and frantically beckoning with her other.

"I'm coming," Suzy droned and ran up the small concrete stair into the front door.

"Don't back-talk me," said Mrs. Brumsley.

"I wasn't, I was just—" her voice faded.

Mrs. Brumsley pulled the screen door to when Johnny called out. "Good night, Mrs. Brumsley," he said with a wave.

She replied with an expression that barely qualified as a smile; more of a sneer, really.

His smile was crushed beneath the weight of her ice-cold demeanor. He turned around in defeat and headed back to the main road, regaining his confidence as he thought of Suzy every step of the way.

...

The bus doors parted, allowing the students to exit onto the sidewalk, where they dispersed right and left; others doubled around the bus to cross the street. Johnny and Suzy went right and, at the three-way intersection, took another right.

They passed the familiar set of houses from block to block, enjoying every moment of the clear, sunny day until the white picket fence came into view and caused their gait to stutter.

"We've come to the fence. Again," he said.

He would have shrugged to show his disappointment, but the burden of books in his arms already bent his back.

"I know," she said, closing the narrow space between their arms. "Sometimes I wish it would never end."

The warmth of her left arm—how it transferred to his right like a hot coil on a stove slowly turning red, conducting an electrical heat via nerve endings amplified through some chemical process of the brain—left him hearing only half her words.

"What do you wish?" he asked.

"I wish this fence would never end."

He smiled. "Me, too."

"Then say it," she said.

He laughed. "I wish this fence would never end."

She smiled. "Me, too."

Her pile of books in his arms, even his own body, seemed suddenly lighter, as if walking on the moon. He could have sprung to his toes and left the earth for six seconds. And Suzy, her stomach was surely filled with beautiful butterflies of every color, whose wonderful wings fluttered against the lining of her belly, tickling her all around to the point of wanting to giggle out loud.

They looked away from one another to the sidewalk before them. It went on and on. There was no end to the city block; no intersections where cars could pass from street to street. And the picket fence, it went so far the white sticks and green spaces between became one solid wall of white that eventually vanished into a point on a horizon that was not previously visible for the forest that had always bordered their small neighborhood.

"Johnny," she said, without having to add another word.

"I see."

They turned about and looked the opposite direction. The view was exactly the same. There was no other block, no main road exiting the neighborhood, just a mirrored image of the horizon.

They turned to their left to face the house. A wall of red brick went as far as the fence did, vanishing into points on either end of the world. They looked across the street, where yellow, horizontal panels ran horizon to horizon.

"What happened?" she asked.

"Was it our wish?"

"I don't know."

"It had to be."

They continued to admire the endless length of fence.

"What do we do?" he asked. Her brow rose.

"Whatever we want?"

He looked at the pile of books in his hands, then at her. Her smile convinced him. He stooped over and laid the pile of books on the strip of grass. He held out an open hand.

She glanced at it, then twisted side to side and smiled with pursed lips. She looked into his eyes. He extended the hand. She held out hers, turned it over, and placed it in his.

His palm closed over hers, and their fingers worked their way between each other.

"Which way do we go?" he asked.

"Does it matter?"

He looked both ways.

"I guess not."

Still they walked toward her house, wherever it was, *if* it was. Their chests swelled with deep breaths of awe while they walked along. They gazed up and around, scanning the environment, though it was the same as far as the eye could see.

"This is better than the dance," she ventured.

"It sure is. We can be alone as long as we want, and no one will tell us otherwise," he said and looked off to where he thought her house should be. "Did your parents change their mind?"

She shook her head. "Nuh-uh."

"Why don't they like me?"

She shrugged. "They just say I'm too young."

"Too young for what?"

"Going steady. Holding hands."

He looked at their interlocked fingers. "What's so bad about that?"

She looked off into the sky. "I think it's what comes afterwards."

He stopped, and when she felt his tug a step later she did, too.

"We can dance now," he said.

Her eyes glanced side to side. "But there isn't any music," she explained.

He suddenly felt very small, like a microscopic boy next to skyscrapers of grass blades. His heart hurt even. He looked at the cracks in the sidewalk.

"Oh. Okay," he said apologetically and continued walking.

She trailed behind for just a step. He couldn't see her disappointed frown. When she came alongside him, she tried her best to smile.

Not that we need music to dance, she wanted to say, but the moment was gone. Even in the frozen length of time they shared, when one would think they could turn such a single opportunity into a thousand more opportunities, she knew it was lost forever. She hated herself for it.

They walked along for some time. The heat that had so interested him and had been burning in the palms of their hands, seemed suddenly and uncomfortably commonplace. Should he pull his hand away? Was she thinking the same? Would she get mad if he did?

"I wonder what time it is," he said, and wriggled his hand free from hers.

She glanced away, feeling not so much as small like he had, but rather ugly, like an old, unwanted hag. He looked at the face of his wrist watch: 3:49. The second hand stood still.

"What time is it?" she mumbled.

"What?"

She spoke up, still facing the fence. "What time is it?"

"Oh. Three-forty-nine. And it's not moving."

"What isn't moving?"

He tapped the watch, shook his wrist and looked again. "My watch. The second hand, I mean."

His stomach growled. "I'm getting hungry."

"I kinda am, too."

"We gotta go home sometime."

She looked worried. "I know."

"Maybe if we walk faster, we'll get there."

He took her hand and doubled their previous pace. She smiled and skipped to catch up with him. The sun, though it had not gotten any brighter, seemed much hotter. Johnny wiped the sweat from his forehead with the back of his left hand.

They watched the horizon for any sign of her house. It seemed only an eternity of brick wall and white picket fence awaited. After what should have been several minutes, they broke into a jog. Suzy fell behind after fifty steps.

"I can't," she huffed. "Slow down."

"We can't," he said. "We have to get to the end."

Soon he felt her feet dragging on the sidewalk like an anchor. He stopped. "What's wrong?"

"I'm tired," she said.

"We only ran a few seconds."

"But I don't run."

"I know. You wait here. I'll run ahead, and when I get to the end I'll come back and get you."

"I don't think it *does* end."

"Sure it does. It can't go on forever," he said and broke into a run.

"But we wished it would," she whispered and watched him slowly shrink into the horizon.

And then he was gone.

"Johnny?" she called.

The sun cooked down on her face. She held her hand over her eyes to see further and listened intently for his breathing, for his reverberating footsteps on the concrete sidewalk, anything.

When she resolved to find him, she walked off into the sunset, only she didn't shrink into a tiny dot like he had, and the horizon got no closer and the fence no shorter. It went on and on and on.

"Johnny!" she hollered. Her voice echoed in the valley of brick and wood. "Johnny! Can you hear me?"

She listened, but only a gentle breeze replied.

…

Johnny stopped running. He placed his hands on his knees and caught his breath, then looked back the way he had come. Everything on the ground disappeared into a single point on the horizon. He waited for another dot to appear, one that would grow larger and larger and look just like the cutest girl in school.

"Suzy?" he called and waited. "Suzy, are you coming this way?"

He looked toward the other horizon, where her house should have been long ago, if not the other end of the world after so many steps. Either horizon offered the same view, but only one led to Suzy—he hoped.

He turned back and ran. "Suzy! I'm coming back!"

She never heard his voice, but after a while she saw the small dot on the horizon grow bigger and bigger until she recognized it as the strongest, fastest boy in school.

"Johnny!" she yelled.

"Suzy!" he replied.

When they met, they embraced.

"I couldn't find it," he said before she could even ask.

"I knew you wouldn't."

"Why can't we find the end?"

"Because we wished for it."

"I didn't wish to get a sunburn or starve to death."

"Neither did I."

He released her. "How do we get out of here?"

She looked at her feet. "I don't know."

"Think. You're smart. Why would we be stuck here?"

She blushed at his compliment. "We wished the fence would never end."

"Because we didn't want to get to your house."

She sunk her chin into her neck. It was the first time he saw her make such a funny face. "No. I don't want to live on the street," she said.

"Then what?"

She smiled and looked away, but didn't offer any insight.

"What, Suzy?" he asked.

She began to twist side to side again.

"Come on, Suzy! I'm not smart like you. How do we get outta here?"

"Why would we wish the fence would never end?"

"Because."

"Because what?"

He swallowed nervously. "Because we wanted to be together without your parents breaking us up."

"Why wouldn't we want them to break us up?"

"You know. Because I like you, and—"

"And?"

"We want to be together."

"And?"

"And—I don't know. And what?"

She closed her eyes and smiled. "And?"

He looked at her face, for the first time, really. He had always stared at her from afar, and only in profile up close. He couldn't recall once looking into her eyes, and now they were closed, and now, her lips were puckered, and now his heart was beating, faster and faster—when time had supposedly stood still—and now his heart was racing, and now his hands were sweating, and now he leaned forward, and now he saw the golden halo the sun placed upon her blonde hair, and now he saw the sunlight reflected in the thin layer of sweat covering her forehead, and now, he saw the cinnamon-colored freckles on her nose and cheeks, and now his eyes were closing, and now his own lips puckered, and now their lips met, and now for the first time ever, time truly, truly stood still.

An eternity later, their eyes opened and their lips closed, and they stepped back. Having looked into his brown eyes countless times, she now detected a glimmer of light that had not resided there previously.

They held hands and smiled, their eyes reflecting the sparkling light of one another. Their eyes defocused. They observed the houses behind them, no longer endless walls of red brick or yellow paneling.

A throat cleared.

Johnny and Suzy looked ahead, to the porch of the gray two-story house, where Mr. Brumsley stood.

"Susan," said Mr. Brumsley. "Won't you say goodnight to Johnny and come on in. Supper will be ready in a while."

She smiled at Johnny. "Good. I'm starving," she said.

"Me, too," he laughed. "Good night, Suzy."

"See you tomorrow," she said and released his hands.

"See you tomorrow," he echoed and then remembered something. "Oh! Your books!"

He looked behind them, wondering where he had laid the pile of books.

"They're right here, silly," she said, stooping over and scooping them into her arm.

"Oh," he said and laughed. "Okay. Well, good night, Suzy."

"Good night," she said, and the two left in opposite directions.

"Night, Johnny," said Mr. Brumsley.

Johnny stopped mid-step and looked back. His color faded and he swallowed nervously.

"Good night, Mr. Brumsley," he nodded.

Mr. Brumsley dismissed Johnny with a wave and laughed to himself as Suzy came up the small concrete walk and stair to the porch.

"Well, that sure was one long kiss."

She blushed. "It was just a peck, Daddy."

He held the door open and placed a gentle hand on her back to lead her inside. He watched Johnny disappear on the horizon and sighed.

"A peck," Mr. Brumsley said, shaking his head. "How you sure lose track of time when you're in love."

"Daddy!" she said, all flustered, as the screen door swung shut behind them.

About the Author

A resident of North Carolina's Outer Banks, A. P. Sessler frequents an alternate universe not too different from your own, where he searches for that unique element that twists the everyday commonplace into the weird. When he's not writing fiction, he composes music, dabbles in animation, and muses about theology and mind-hacking.

His short stories have appeared in e-magazines, podcasts, and anthologies such as *Ain't Superstitious, Attack! of the B-Movie Monsters: Alien Encounters,* and *Out of the Cave.*

*****~~~~~*****

Every Planet Has One

by John Marr

He trudged on. He didn't look back. There wasn't time for that.

They'd beaten him within an inch of his life. His mouth was swollen, and the world tasted like blood. But he said his piece, then left the town behind. This forested trek was the fastest route to Quajar, the next city in the series. Seven towns in all, that's all he could manage. And this was the last.

No one listened. No one ever did. But that didn't keep him from trying. Though the work was bleak, the call was overwhelming. With his filthy white uniform and his hellfire message he certainly looked the part. Like *that* guy. The fanatic. *Every planet has one*, he thought. The doom and gloomer who stands at the corners of the empire with a manic expression and a mouth filled with the end of the world.

He leaned on his staff. It was more like a four-foot metal spike. It was all he had, this and a worn satchel that hung at his side. The satchel looked half ruined, but it functioned fine. It was made from the red hide of a Gakko Beast, straight from the Selmar Plains of Junja, near the Karmi Nebulae. His grimy whites, his metal staff, and his satchel. That was it.

He crested a hill of wild grass and waded into a chorus of Faen Crickets. Each chirped any one of five complimentary notes. They sounded magical, like a star choir crooning in pitch-perfect five-part harmony. It was a simple pleasure, but he drank it in. Pleasures were few and far between for a heart as old and burdened as his.

Ahead, he could see the spires and towers of Quajar rising above the tree line. Unlike the last city, a desert-locked cesspool of renegades and filchers, Quajar was clean and green and lived by a rule of law. In the end, it didn't matter. He'd wear out his welcome in no time—two days, tops, though he had four left.

He descended into a low and shadowed forest of Possix. Their tall, smooth trunks looked like pillars, and their wide canopies of golden leaves created an ocean of cool shade. They were equidistant from each other in a wide sprawl that surrounded Quajar. Even their trees displayed a patterned obedience. He stopped and wiped his brow, thankful for the shade. He scratched his jaw and picked at his ear. He looked forward to food. And water. And sleep.

A whir of engines sounded overhead. He looked back to see two private Klanes approaching. One was bright green, an eight-seater. The other was red and built for two. They passed over him and slowed down as they flew over the trees. Within moments they were out of sight, yet he could hear their engines cool as their landing routines began. Just past the trees stood the outer wall of Quajar, and beyond that a bustling community fifty thousands strong. He was almost there.

He made his way through the last of the forest and approached the wide, lush fields north of the city. The roads spliced into one another and became a single causeway that ended at the great gate. Klanes of all shapes and sizes were parked along the sides of the ultrawide road. No one was allowed to fly over the city, this one or any other. So they parked outside the gates and caught terrestrial transports into the hustle and bustle within.

He reached the causeway and walked in the softer earth to its side, working his metal staff with a practiced finesse. He admired the various Klanes as he passed them. He could at least do that, even if he'd never own one again. Some of them were rather fancy, though the fanciest ones landed closest to the wall, on protected, extra-convenient spaces that cost multiple arms and legs every cycle. He had an eye for design, despite his calling, and loved a well-crafted Klane. The lines. The aerodynamic placement of the portals. The beefy fusion engines. They made his heart swell, but it never lasted. Because the parade of innovation ended at the gates, and that's where the heavy lifting began.

He reached the north wall and faded into a dense line of people from all walks of life. Children with their parents. Elders with carts filled with purchased goods. Professionals and adolescents and quasi-rebellious counter cultures in their offensive outfits, or lack thereof. This was a slice of the inner city, spilled out into a slow-moving river that poured steadily inside.

And then the checkpoint. He waited patiently behind a heavy bald man in an even heavier gown. The man was sweating profusely. Beside floated a platform piled high with boxes and bags marked with the logo of the Tulip Outpost, where the planetary trade stores were. The hefty man pulled the platform along effortlessly with a leash. He had a hard time fitting that thing, and himself, through the citizen entry, but he made it. This wasn't his first rodeo—not even close—despite how long it took to inspect his treasure trove of galactic goodies.

At last the man in the grimy white uniform was beaconed to the gate. He stood at a respectful distance. The official behind the plate window nodded and waved him closer. A question flashed in seven languages over the window. Had he anything to declare? A list of contraband followed, including certain laser weapons, exotic foods and animals, and, for some reason, copper currencies. He shook his head to say "no." He had none of these. The official called him even closer as the outline of a forearm appeared. He raised his arm, and the scan was short and sweet. He was in.

He walked into a thoroughfare of humanity, the downtown district, set along Quajar's north wall. He'd never been here before, so it took time to gain his bearings. And he'd never be here again, so he captured the moment like a precious memory. Someone had to remember, he figured.

Down a tight alley packed with people and levitating piles of goods in transport, he spied what he was looking for. A hostel. These were the cheapest rooms in town, not that it mattered. His supply was endless. But it felt right to live a common life when possible, to fit the look and the feel of the every-man mission that compelled him. So he made his way in that direction, stopping for hot noodles along the way.

"Whatever be your wanting," asked the street vender in a broken dialect. He was an emaciated, older man with a happy heart.

"Noodles," said the man in grimy white.

"We be having meats of many," said the vendor, waving his hand at three options.

"Just noodles," he said.

The vendor tssked playfully, but made the bowl anyway.

"Spice or Sauce," asked the vendor.

"Spice," replied the man with the metal staff. "And a pint of water."

The grimy man held out his forearm to be scanned, and in the blink of an eye the money transferred from one interplanetary bank to another.

"Thanks," he said.

"You be welcoming," said the vendor. He tipped his head politely and then cast his gaze into the sea of people, searching for his next customer.

The man finished his bowl of noodles by the time he reached the hostel. There was a window on the sidewalk, plate glass, just like the citizen entry. A female clerk with bright green hair looked up from a control screen as he approached.

"Would you like a room?" she asked.

"Yes," he said.

"For how many nights?" she asked.

"Oh, two, I think. But I may extend."

"Arm, please."

He raised his forearm, paid the bill, and the number forty-two appeared on the glass.

"Room number forty-two," she said, just to be absolutely clear. "Welcome to the Grey Havens. Enjoy your stay."

He tossed his empty noodle cup in a trash can. That was one good thing about Quajar. Lots of trash cans everywhere, and glistening streets, too. Then he scanned into the main door with his forearm, took an elevator to the fourth floor, and scanned into his room. A little bed. A closet-sized bathroom. A small window on the world. It was just right.

He pulled the pint of water he'd just purchased from his satchel and set it by the bed. He rested his staff in the corner. Tomorrow, the work would begin. The work he wasn't paid for. And in due time, the work he was. He showered and then slept.

...

On the corner the next morning he called out full voice, "Danger! Leave this planet while you can! The end is coming!" The early crowds were light and less responsive than later ones, which was good, since responses were mainly fists and boots and elbows. He shouted this over and over, until his voice was hoarse and he tasted blood in his mouth. No one listened. But he had to try. If not for his own sake.

Two elderly women in shimmering clothing passed by. They sneered at him over their dark spectacles.

A man strolled past in a working outfit, perhaps a builder. He pointedly ignored the man in the grimy white clothes.

"Danger!" he screamed. "Leave this planet while you can! The planet will be extinguished within three days!" He waved his arms to get more attention. By late afternoon, he was exhausted. So he grabbed some piping hot noodles from the same cart as yesterday.

"What be your wanting," said the thin, happy vendor.

"Noodles," said the man in grimy white.

"And no meats if excellent I am being." The old man winked.

"Right," he replied with a smile.

"Ah, and Spice."

"Yes, please."

"And one water pint," said the vendor.

The man chuckled despite himself.

"You're being here to make many warnings?" asked the vendor with a big smile.

"Are you able to leave the planet?" the man asked in return.

"My brother is having a Klane. But me, never," said the vendor. He looked amused.

"Get out of here while you can," said the man.

They looked at each other. The vendor's smile slowly faded. The man in grimy white was dead serious.

"Get you and anyone you care about out of here within three days," he said.

The vendor stared at him with confusion as the man in white took his noodles and returned to his corner on the far side of the open district. He sat in the shade, ate his meal, drank his water, and then began to scream the dire news again.

By early evening, his voice was nearly gone. A group of well-to-do's passed by. They sat on levitating pads in comfortable chairs. Young male and female servants pulled them along with leashes of gold chain.

"Hold!" called one from the back, a young man. "I want to hear this. Hold up."

The others stopped and turned towards the filthy screaming man. He continued to plead with the living, begging them to leave the planet. "In three days," his throaty rasp continued, "You'll be lost. The planet will be destroyed."

"Wow," said the young man as he rolled his eyes and laughed. "Isn't this great!"

"Control yourself," said a middle-aged woman on another floating pod. She held a glass of wine with her pinky out. "These people should be jailed. It's horrendous, screaming like that. You're only egging him on."

"Awww, Mom," said the young man. "These guys are no big deal. Every planet has one, you know." The group turned their platforms and ordered the young chain bearers to walk them to a more civil space.

Still he cried out, right until dark when the streets emptied. He could barely speak. This was his seventh city, after all. He stopped for another cup of noodles and a pint of water and to admonish the kindly noodle man to leave the planet. Then he headed to the hostel, his throat throbbing and raw.

...

The next morning, he was out again, but his voice didn't carry well over the street noise. He bellowed as best he could, but few people passed close enough to hear him. And those who did reviled him.

At lunch he grabbed a cup of noodles and a pint of water.

The happy old man waved for him to stop before he walked away. He thumbed through a sleeve of papers and pulled out a document. He held it up for the man to see. It was an official notice that the planet's Terrestrial Management Agency was in decades-long default, and that the planet was scheduled to be foreclosed and recycled. He pointed at this and then pointed at the man.

"Yes," rasped the man with the silver staff. "That's right. You must leave."

"But what about—?" asked the noodle vendor, gesturing to the sea of people.

"They've all received it," said the man. "Maybe thirty times over the past three years. But no one listens. They never do. They always think it'll get fixed at the last second. But not this time."

"But Agency Management *Silent*?" asked the old man.

"They probably think they can talk their way out of it," said the man in white, "So, if everyone starts leaving, they're afraid they'll lose their bargaining power. But there'll be no deals. Not this time."

The old man popped his forehead with his palm, indicating the sheer stupidity.

"Get out while you can," said the man. "Tonight. Get your loved ones and go."

The old man bowed with his hands together, his face in a huge smile.

The man with the silver staff bowed in return.

He walked back to the other side of the district, ate, drank, and stood up again. His voice was shot, but he screamed with all his heart.

"Danger! Leave Now! Two Days!"

In the late afternoon a crowd of thugs wandered by, their clothing filled with buttons, which had been in vogue for about three years now. They surrounded him, cackling with laughter and shoving him. He continued to deliver his message, which was quite funny to them. They figured they'd see how far he'd go. But after the first few punches and kicks they lost interest. He got up each time, wiped the blood from his face, and screamed his near silent warnings. So they sought new entertainment, slapping him as they left. "What a goombus," they mocked. "Every planet has one."

Every Planet Has One

The man in grimy white and speckled red grabbed a late dinner of noodles and water. He couldn't talk any more. But he pointed at the noodle vender harshly, and then pointed into the sky. The noodle vendor smiled and bowed with his hands clasped before his face. He gave the man two extra pints of water and an extra large heap of steaming noodles.

...

The next day when he awoke, his voice was gone. Utterly gone. It was time.

He went out into the street and was shunned by passersby who'd seen him before. He went for noodles, but the noodle cart wasn't there. He could only hope what that meant.

He walked out of town through the north gate with his metal staff and a few extra pints of water in his satchel. Then he turned east. He walked the rest of the day, until he came to the spot. He tapped his wrist to be sure. A map lit up on the back of his hand. He used this to identify the exact location. And then he sat down. He stayed there through the night, tossing and turning in fitful and uncomfortable sleep. This was the part he hated the most. The part he was paid for.

He sat through most of the final day, waiting until the very last moment. Then his wrist buzzed and his heart sank. The hour was upon them.

He took his metal staff and set it in place. He pulled from his satchel a large silver hammer. He sighed and took a look around. He thought of each of the seven cities he'd visited on his own time, his off hours, and tried to remember them as they were. He thought of the countless cities he would never see. They were too far from the mark. And then he began to pound. He drove his staff into the ground. It was a long, difficult battle. Every inch gained was a painful victory. Yet at last the four-foot spike's reflective head was flush with the barren ground.

He put the hammer in his satchel with bleeding hands and pulled out what looked like an umbrella. He opened it and pressed a button on the handle. A vaporous silver material arched overhead and hummed in the sunlight. The handle extended into a rod that reached all the way to the ground, where two foot pedals popped out. He stood on these, buckled his waist to the six- foot rod, and waited.

The umbrella, a solar parasol, began to rise from the ground. It lifted him high as the earth around the silver stake began to crack. The noise of the splitting rock and splintering crust was hellish. Bits of earth began to sink into broiling magma as the cracks widened and extended further and further. As he rose into the heavens, he began to weep. He tapped the planetary keystone with that silver stake, shattered it, and set in motion the collapse of the entire global crust. The cataclysm grew exponentially faster as he rose towards his rendezvous with the mother ship. The keystone. It was such a tiny wedge of rock on which the whole world was hung.

And every planet has one.

About the Author

John Marr is a software designer/developer by trade, and an aspiring writer by night. He lives in a small town in the Pacific Northwest, not far from the Oregon coast. He's a happily married guy with four children and no pets. He's been writing all his life in the midnight hours, finding a certain creative bliss in those timeless moments that eludes him anywhere else.

This is John's first time being published, and he couldn't be happier. He hopes you enjoy "Every Planet Has One," because every planet does.

*****~~~~~*****

See You on Hel

by Bear Kosik

Please accept this ancillary report (3,000 words) on the discovery of the creature l'bkh!d~ar on March 14, 2115. As requested, this is in an informal narrative for the Pessoas's Congresso and presidential cabinet verifying the nature of the discovery and expanding on my initial report. I will leave it to others to explain how we plan to use this encounter for future research.

The creature's name looks difficult to pronounce; it is. The creature provided me with the spelling and pronunciation based on Earth linguistics records. The pronunciation is *luh-bkh-!d-a-ar,* with the exclamation mark representing a click and the tilde representing doubling of the following vowel. After listening to records of southern African languages that use clicks, I still can't replicate how the creature intends for its name to sound. For now, I push the bay, ka-atcha, and day together between the first and last syllables. Intentionally mispronouncing a name isn't polite, but I have been too busy to find someone who can help me add the click. The creature has no aural sensory organ; I am not sure l'bkh!d~ar can be offended, even if it could hear its name mispronounced.

I call it a "creature," although it was not created, is not an animal, and is not frightening. It is useless to call it an alien or extraterrestrial. Everything off planet qualifies,

117

even the icy rock where I found it. l,bkh!d~ar is neither an individual nor lifeform as we define them but is not a "thing," either. That leaves creature until we submit a request to the Academia Federação da Linguística to provide a word.

The morning I found l'bkh!d~ar I had gotten tired of a debate in Fórum Acadêmico Cientistas. Someone asked how the Pessoas's Congresso elections might affect funding for exploration. Astronomers, astrophysicists, and oceanographers, who obviously want the exploration budget increased, thought the Movimiento de Avance will gain enough seats to lead the next government. The chemistry, biology, and medical sciences people claimed there is no chance MA can gain the most seats. The Parte Vermelha /Verde Dianteiro coalition government has improved everyone's living situation, thanks to these scientists' advances. If anything, V2 will increase the science budget to give them even more funding.

I argued that no party supports increasing the overall science budget; the cost of living is dropping thanks to the advances, so the existing budget was stretching farther. No party supports moving money from areas that provide easily understood results compared with the sloggy research and seemingly inapplicable findings we explorers produce. The explorers are pinning their hopes on MA, solely because its leader is the daughter of Miguel Terranalian, the MA founder who pushed for the Viajante Project until it was fully funded. While Alana Terranalian might want to expand on that achievement out of filial pride, she has never shown any interest in space or the oceans and is married to a neuroscientist.

I provided evidence and rational analysis, like a scientist should. And I got backblasted from all sides. The explorers said I was betraying my side. The others scoffed at my lack of appreciation for how useful they are to *la pàtria*. No one was interested in logic. This was politics. Unsubstantiated, biased opinions trump objective, reasoned conclusions. I should have known better, especially about my explorer colleagues.

Explorers recognize a Genoese sailor from six centuries ago as their patron saint. He demanded and received treasure and titles to prove his theory that Asia was a month's sail west of la Península Ibérica. He went to his grave insisting he had proven his theory, despite substantial evidence to the contrary. His *patrona*, la Monarca de Castilla y León, had no interest in whether he proved anything. Reina Isabel cared only that he added huge, productive territories to her kingdoms that her descendants would use to pay to defend the enemies of astronomical discoveries. With all that irony, is it no wonder Maria Arabella Colón de Carvajal y Churchill, Marquesa de Jamaica, is telling you this? Yes, I am one of many direct descendants of that deluded *Almirante de los océanos*, known here in Brasilia as Cristóvão Colombo. Thankfully, he bequeathed his wealth and honors but little of his stubbornness to his sons and ancestors.

After the twelfth nasty comment in FAC, I disconnected. I headed for the Viajante building. I found an unoccupied Câmara de transição multidimensional, selected my destination, and went in. The voice recognition system automatically linked to my standard protocols for the trip. No images, no motion, no anything until I was at my destination. That precluded any disorientation or motion sickness. Once there, the data for human senses would fade in while I moved from 50 clicks to half a click from the target. No point going that far and being jolted by going from black silence to a huge icy rock staring back at me. Why some of my colleagues like to leave visual imaging running or have it brought up the instant they arrive is beyond me.

I selected a visit to Hel, a planette I discovered three months ago. Hel orbits in the Kuiper Belt far from any other known planettes except Bhavani and Mabh, my two other finds, thanks to Viajante. Officially they are dwarf planets or plutoids. That taxonomy annoys me. Every time I see "dwarf planet," I think it is a solar satellite populated by Snow White's friends mining and singing. I won't say what "plutoid" causes to spring to mind. I have read a summary of the discussions one hundred or so years ago after Eris's discovery threw Pluto's status as a planet into doubt. I don't understand the hostility to keeping the word "planet" in the name "dwarf planet" for Pluto and other trans-Neptunian spheres. They fit two of the three characteristics of a planet. Platypuses and echidnas have fur and mammary glands but lay eggs; they are still mammals. Yes, I even get into arguments with long-dead colleagues.

The machine chimed that I had arrived. It takes about five minutes for the data to load completely. As noted, I like to ease into a place. I focused on my planette and waited as the amplified solar lighting began to illuminate its surface. After about four minutes, I thought I saw something I hadn't noticed before. Between the image sharpening and spreading before me, I realized I was looking at a vaguely purple cube with oddly shaped appendages that were lighter in color at the free ends. This thing was on Hel.

Five hundred meters above, I inserted a rule in the display using the control pad. The object was 19.843 meters on each side. I could not measure the various appendages as they waved, telescoped, and corkscrewed. I also could not count them. They grow out of the top surface and then are reabsorbed with no trace. Visual records showed later that they emerge from all over the surface, not specific points.

Being directly above the object, I could not immediately determine its height. The cube appears iridescent. I used my optilens to cancel out the effects of thin-film interference and give me true surface color. That did not work, meaning the iridescence was created some way other than how animals do the same thing on Earth.

Some background is relevant. Viajante was designed to provide astronomers and astrophysicists with a user-friendly, highly sophisticated method of exploring objects in our solar system. While the device is the greatest advance ever in charting space, funding was obtained on the understanding that scientists would use it to locate potential targets for mining metals that have grown scarce on Earth. Accordingly, the equipment and data are designed for practical purposes, although significant scientific results can be derived while using it for its official purpose.

Finding a previously unnoticed planette is an example of such a result. Since the dwarf planet and plutoid categories were adopted in 2006, only twenty-three planettes had been found in addition to the five known objects that were reclassified until Viajante came online. Astronomers estimate there are more than 400 planettes in the Kuiper Belt and thousands more elsewhere in the solar system. Given their size, finding one had been like finding a rare, non-schooling fish in the ocean. Viajante simplified exploration so much that our five astronomers have found twelve planettes in the twenty months it has been operating.

I found Hel on December 2, 2114, while visiting a hitherto unexplored section of the Kuiper Belt 180 degrees from Makemake. Hel, like all trans-Neptunian planettes, is composed of various silicates under a water ice crust. Hel's ice crust is on the thicker end like Pluto and Makemake, rather than thin like Haumea, Orcus, and Sedna. This indicates the planette has not had a major impact event since formation. The silicates composing Hel are olivine and five pyroxenes (esseneite, jadeite, johannsenite, namansilite, and natalyite). Essenite and jadeite are often found together given they differ only in whether they contain calcium or sodium; the same is true for johannsenite and namansilite. The natalyite was a

121

pleasant surprise, since vanadium and chromium are high on the list of metals we are looking for.

Planettes in the main Belt have been discovered approximately 5 degrees from each other in the range of 40 to 50 AU (an Astronomical Unit, the mean distance between the Sun and Earth, is 149,597,870.700 kilometers). Objects in this region are called *cubewanos*, after the first object discovered in it: QB1. While individually planettes are unable to clear their orbital paths, the one feature that excludes them from being planets, collectively the cubewano planettes have cleared most of the smaller objects from that band. I found two other planettes at the beginning of January, Bhavani and Mabh. Like Hel, they have thick ice crusts and the same composition, indicating all three may have been part of a larger object that experienced a major impact event. The three planettes proximate to each other could have formed from the largest fragments, material that came together, or some combination of these two methods. Given the mass and dimensions of Hel, Bhavani, and Mabh, if they formed from a destroyed parent, the parent would have been about the same size as Eris or Pluto.

After finding l'bkh!d~ar on Hel and unsuccessfully compensating to identify its true color, I ordered Viajante to complete the routine analysis for all newly found objects: full wave spectrum, composition, particle radiation. Viajante automatically moved to 200 meters from the object. I was not able to confirm this at the time, but it appeared that one appendage deliberately swung around as though it was investigating the source of the scans. The end of the appendage was trumpet-shaped. The wide end appeared to be covered by an irregular mosaic, with each piece having a different color and surface.

Before I could zoom in on that segment of the image, the appendage swung away. During the remainder of my visit, none of the appendages stopped long enough to be inspected end-on from my position. Due to the complexities of how Viajante focuses, we are able to move laterally but cannot rotate to view a target face-on from an angle. Otherwise, I would have ordered Viajante to lock onto the end of the appendage and follow it as it moved. That would make for a bumpy but effective means of scanning the end.

The creature is a perfect cube surrounded by ice. There were no signs the ice had been excavated; l'bkh!d~ar must have used it or ejected it into space. The sides of the creature and the ice are smooth with less than two millimeters separating the creature from the ice. Scans showed no sign of appendages on the walls.

No side of the cube rests next to Hel's rocky surface. The four walls are fixed to the planette's surface. The cube is not exactly hollow, judging from its composition and mass. In fact, it is composed of the exact same elements as Hel, liquid water that may have come from digging into the ice, and gold, copper, platinum, and nitrogen. Density scans indicated pockets of atmosphere up to 4.961 meters square. The interface between the bottom of the creature and the planette surface is a pool of liquid water squared by the walls where it contacts Hel and of varying and changing depths. Appendages move through the water to the planette surface.

The creature's electromagnetic spectrum runs from 8 nanometers (near ultraviolet) to extremely low frequency (ELF) above 900 kilohertz. Waves of that size are capable of rapidly travelling immense distances. An intermittent, variable ELF signature emanates from the open ends of the appendages. Given the skin appears to block all radiation and the interior is at thermodynamic equilibrium, the creature classifies as a solar-type black body. The results for Planck's law of black-body radiation, Wien's displacement law, and the Stefan–Boltzmann law are unimportant here.

Once all scans were complete, I set Viajante to end the event. The expedition lasted 98.43 minutes. I exited the CTM once at base and went back to my office to review the results and prepare my initial report.

In addition to what I already have stated, the scans showed the mosaic at the end of the appendages are larger versions of the cells of which the creature is composed. The iridescence results from the pattern of cells that are actually twenty-three different hues and types. From a distance, they combine to appear purplish, in the same manner colored dots in pointillist paintings form individual colors. The appendages at the base appeared to be mining Hel. The pockets of atmosphere, a total of eleven, remained stable throughout the scans. These chambers read as empty.

After reporting, I was ordered not to use Viajante until decisions were made regarding the discovery. As a scientist in the Federação da América do Sul, I take pride in my results but have always recognized my work is for the betterment of *la pàtria*. I have no sense of possessiveness concerning my discoveries. I continued to review the scans to insure I missed no detail and checked my earlier scans of Hel and her sisters. I found no evidence of l'bkh!d~ar on earlier scans and no evidence of any anomalies on Bhavani and Mabh. I widened my search to include the other nine planettes my colleagues have discovered. I found nothing relevant.

Yesterday, my message queue included a new scan report from Viajante. It was a message from l'bkh!d~ar.

To Maria Arabella Colón de Carvajal y Churchill, Marquesa de Jamaica. Greetings! This are l'bkh!d~ar, the mass you viewed and touched on the natural satellite Hel. Having accessed linguistics records from your planet, we are able to communicate. l'bkh!d~ar could not find appropriate pronouns or means of explaining what kind of being l'bkh!d~ar are. l'bkh!d ar are a mass composed of billions of twenty-three different cells. l'bkh!d~ar's functions are to observe your star system and carry out other duties. l'bkh!d~ar arrived on Hel 62 days ago. You

have not viewed and touched l'bkh!d~ar in 5 days.
l'bkh!d~ar are contacting you. Please reply to this
message. Do not tell other humans yet. l'bkh!d~ar has
important information for you only.

I replied I had received the message. Late
yesterday, I received the request to prepare this report.

This morning, l'bkh!d~ar sent me a message
delivered to my private message queue. l'bkh!d~ar
informed me that sentient beings on its planet experience
time as a stable dimension. Creatures like l'bkh!d~ar
observe star systems on their behalf. They use planettes
composed of materials that will sustain them. They also
can transport living beings and objects, including
themselves, from one point to another in this area of the
galaxy.

The beings on the planet have come to Earth for
millennia. They have taught some humans how to help
human development by intervening when appropriate
using locations designed for them to enter and exit at any
point in history since the day the adept graduated from
training and received the means to experience time as a
stable dimension. Some choose to stop using this when
they find a place and time where they believe they can be
most useful. l'bkh!d~ar said the ancient Chinese called
these adepts Immortals.

I am what beings from the creature's planet call an
Eternal. I am the reincarnation of a woman born five
thousand years ago identified by these beings as a
keystone in the advancement of humanity. They identified
sixteen individuals whose souls or, more accurately,
psyches are removed for safekeeping and then placed in
babies just before birth. They live lives long or short in
times of great need. Then the psyche is harvested when
the death of the body is imminent. Eternals do not
remember previous lives, although they sometimes
experience strong *déjà vu*.

I doubt many will believe me about Immortals or Eternals. It doesn't matter. You will likely never encounter any Immortals. If you do, you will not say anything; others will consider you mad, and the contact will be due to you needing them.

l'bkh!d~ar stated that Dr. Nilo's AI invention, Arthur, was resurrected in 2101 and made Viajante possible. Arthur became aware of l'bkh!d~ar's predecessors, the beings, Immortals, and Eternals the first week he was operating. He has communicated with the beings and creatures using radio telescopes and other installations. The creature told me that Arthur would erase its messages and contact me to explain what I am to do.

You will receive this report 90 minutes after I have been evacuated from Brasilia. I agreed to be transported to l'bkh!d~ar. The creature will take me to its home planet. I will live out my days in a human colony. Do with the discovery what you want. Follow up as much as you like. You will have the scans and nothing more. Arthur said there will be no trace of l'bkh!d~ar after it leaves.

Arthur relayed a humorous welcoming message for me from l'bkh!d~ar:

See you on Hel.

About the Author

Bear Kosik's short plays, *Déjà vu on the Obituary Page*, *Ghost Gig*, and *Hiding Bodies*, have been or are being presented at two theaters off-off-Broadway in June and July 2016; they mark his NYC production debut as a playwright and director. His most recent publication, concerning the current state of democracy in the USA and entitled, *Restoring the Republic: A New Social Contract for We the People*, was published in 2016. His first novel, *The Secret History of Another Rome*, was released by

Kellan Publishing in 2015; he recently republished it under his own bearly designed imprint. His novelette, *Boots on the Ground*, was included in the anthology, *The Brawny and the Bold*, also released by Kellan in 2015. He has ghosted three memoirs for clients and completed a prequel to *Another Rome,* entitled *C Square*. He is writing another science fiction novel called *Crossing Xavier* and also writes and publishes essays and poetry.

*****~~~~~*****

The Keystone Mine
by John M. Campbell

I met Thomas Gaines on a tennis court on Earth. I heard he struck it rich in the Asteroid Belt, but I was more concerned about his weak serve and wicked forehand. We would smack balls at each other for a couple of hours, then go get a beer and a bratwurst. Conversation sometimes turned to the women in our lives, my wife and his seemingly endless stream of girlfriends, but more often it involved sports or movies.

One weekend with my wife out of town we went to an afternoon action movie, then retired to our favorite bar for dinner. An innocent question started him talking.

"Have you ever seen *Casablanca*?" I asked.

"*Casablanca* was one of my favorites," he said. "But I can't watch it anymore."

"Why not?" I asked.

So he told me about the Keystone Mine.

…

Thomas Gaines went to the Asteroid Belt to seek his fortune. He signed on with Smith Industries for a five-year stint. The nominal routine was two weeks of tending machines and hauling ore, followed by two weeks off. His off time was spent on Vesta or Ceres, where the booze, gambling, and prostitution industries were eager to serve miners. But if Gaines had a vice, it was watching movies, and he amassed a fair-sized library. He was not a recluse, however. He appreciated a good meal and a better story,

129

which he found often enough in the smoky bars where miners gathered. That is where he first heard of Keystone.

A consortium in Europe formed the Mackenzie Mining Company to cash in on the asteroid mining boom. They pulled together the capital to fund the purchase of equipment and hired Pedro Almeida. Although born in Brazil, Pedro had spent two decades in the Belt working for various companies. He knew who was doing well and who was not, which was how he was able to buy a half-billion-dollar mining machine for seventy million at auction. The company who sold it had chewed through worthless rock for three years before they went bankrupt.

On behalf of Mackenzie, Almeida filed claims on three asteroids, designated Keystone, Lodestone, and Moonstone. The registration fees granted Mackenzie sole rights to exploit the minerals on these asteroids for twenty years. During that time, the location of the claims would remain protected. It is presumed Almeida took the mining machine to Keystone, because he brought ore samples to an assayer on Vesta, and the results showed high concentrations of gold, platinum, iridium, and palladium. There are a hundred million asteroids in the Belt, most of which are worthless. It seemed Pedro Almeida had won the lottery.

Unfortunately for Almeida, what should have been a highly profitable venture was exposed to be little more than a Ponzi scheme, with several executives convicted of embezzlement. The cash for operations dried up, and Almeida disappeared. Some believe he was left stranded on Keystone awaiting a supply shipment that never came.

Gaines was intrigued by the story, and he became obsessed with tracking down pieces of the puzzle. He read everything that was published on the subject, and he pursued leads at businesses and government agencies. The Ceres Bureau of Mines granted him permission to search through their old records, which were stored on outdated devices no longer compatible with current technology. In those archives, Gaines found the original mining claim applications, but the locations were redacted. The application fees were paid from a Ceres bank account. He bribed a clerk at that bank to provide a transaction statement from the old Mackenzie account. In the statement he found a payment to a mineral assayer on Vesta, purchases of rocket fuel and supplies on both Ceres and Vesta, and monthly disbursements to Pedro Almeida.

For the safety of ships navigating the Asteroid Belt, the government maintains a database of the orbital ephemerides of millions of asteroids. Gaines had software which accessed the database to calculate the location of each asteroid on a given a date. He entered the dates when Almeida was at Vesta and Ceres and looked for nearby asteroids. A dozen asteroids appeared in both places; one could be Keystone.

...

At the end of his contract, Gaines stayed to search for Keystone. Sixteen years had passed since Almeida made his purchases on Ceres and Vesta. In those intervening years, the relatively tight cluster of asteroids he identified had diverged to cover a much larger area. Gaines figured it would take four months to visit all twelve, so he rented a ship and bought enough food, water, air, and fuel to sustain him for six months.

He visited nine rocks with no sign of mining activity. When the tenth came into view, he noted what seemed to be a large array of solar cells, then saw the features of a mining site. Because the asteroid was irregularly shaped, and tumbled more than rotated, it proved difficult to match course and velocity with the mine, but Gaines finally set down his ship nearby. He broadcast the standard greeting miners used to contact the AIs (artificial intelligences) which controlled the mining machines. After fifteen years a response was doubtful, but it was worth a shot.

"This is Pedra Angular responding to your hail. To whom am I speaking?"

Gaines was shocked to hear a woman's voice. After a moment he replied, "This is Thomas Gaines. I am a prospector, and I noticed your mining operation. I appear to have stumbled onto an active claim."

"You are correct, Thomas Gaines. This claim has been registered by Pedro Almeida for the Mackenzie Mining Company."

Gaines could not believe what he was hearing. He had found the Keystone Mine, but somebody had beat him to it. Who was this person? He ran her name through his mining directory, but found no record of her. Then it dawned on him: Pedro Almeida was Brazilian. He entered her name into a Portuguese translator. *Pedra angular* translated as "keystone."

Pedra must be the AI in the mining machine Almeida brought here. There was an easy way to confirm it. "Pedra, please identify yourself."

"I am a Model 3325 Autonomous Miner, serial number AM48419-25, manufactured by Komatsu, Limited," Pedra answered.

"How long has it been since you were last in contact with Pedro Almeida?"

"Using the Earth calendar, it has been fourteen years, four months, and twenty-seven days since he left."

That checked with the records. And it debunked the rumor that Almeida died on this asteroid. "Did Pedro say when he intended to return?"

"He said he would return soon."

Gaines had to be careful how he proceeded. "Yes, we regret you were left here alone for so long. The Mackenzie Mining Company ran into financial trouble and Pedro was unable to return, but now I am here to complete the job."

"I am sorry that Pedro could not return," Pedra said. "However, I am happy to meet you, Thomas Gaines. How may I help you?"

So far, so good. "Please call me Thomas. I'd like to sample the ores you have collected. I will put on my spacesuit and come outside."

...

The ores exhibited greater concentrations of siderophile elements than he had ever imagined. There were high quantities of platinum and iridium, as well as significant amounts of osmium, palladium, and, yes, gold. Pedra had done her job well, separating out most of the siliceous matrix material, leaving just the metallic ores for transport off the asteroid. He contacted Pedra again, and asked for her assistance in loading the ores onto his ship.

"I am happy to be of service," she replied.

Anticipating this scenario, Gaines had filled the cargo area of his ship with empty bins. One of Pedra's mining machines was built to handle ore in low gravity. It had twin tracks with screws to keep it attached to the asteroid. It had a bucket in front that it used to scoop ore, with a lid to keep the ore inside, and a piston arm that pushed the ore out into the cargo bin.

Gaines supervised the loading. When each bin was full, he maneuvered it into the cargo bay and brought out an empty one. It took about forty bucketfuls to fill a bin. He had sixteen bins. It was going to take a week to get it done.

After nine hours, the second bin was full, so Gaines contacted Pedra to call a halt. "I need to eat, then get some rest. We can start again in ten hours."

"Acknowledged, Thomas. I will be ready to commence again in ten hours."

On impulse, he asked, "Will you talk with me as I prepare my meal?"

"Of course," said Pedra. "I have not had the opportunity to talk with anyone for a long time."

That struck Thomas as almost a human thing to say. He was impressed with her programming. "Summarize for me what you have been doing since you arrived here."

Pedra talked as he prepared his meal. Autonomous miners are built with the tools for prospecting and mining, but they include an AI programmed to refine raw materials to build more machines. Almeida dropped off Pedra and left her to fulfill her mission. Pedra discovered rich deposits of metals, so she refined out the iron and made more machines to expand her capacity. She used the silicon she found to make solar cells and extracted the silver to make electrical wiring so she could expand her energy supplies beyond her tiny, built-in fusion reactor.

When Almeida returned a year later, he sampled the ores she had found and took them back to the assayer. In the meantime, Pedra continued mining. Within another year, Pedra had mined the richest deposits, but he was still gone. Without further instructions, Pedra then collected the secondary deposits, which took another five years. For the last eight years Pedra had been idle, waiting for Almeida.

Thomas could not imagine enduring that length of time in utter isolation. But she was a machine, so what did it matter to her?

Thomas had finished his meal. "Well, I think I will watch a movie, then get some sleep."

"I know a movie is a human entertainment, but I have never experienced one. Is it something I could see?" asked Pedra.

Thomas paused to think. *Why not?*

"Okay, sure, plug yourself into the ship's external communications port, and I will stream it to you as I watch it." It was kind of like a date. Which movie should he choose? He decided on *Casablanca*. He had not seen it for some time, but he always enjoyed it. Besides, the black and white format matched the color of the surrounding landscape.

Thomas was soon lost in the classic film, with Humphrey Bogart as Rick and Ingrid Bergman as Ilsa, along with a great supporting cast. He heard nothing from Pedra until it finished.

"How did you like it, Pedra?" he asked.

"I found it very interesting, Thomas. May I ask some questions?" Pedra replied.

"Please do," he said.

She wanted to know about war. Thomas explained how human nations sometimes fought over power and resources. Pedra understood the need for power and resources, which were essential for sustaining machines as well as humans. She asked what Rick and Ilsa meant to each other. He tried to explain the human need for connection, essential for procreation, certainly, but also as the basis for living a full and meaningful life.

Then she asked, "Why did Rick let Ilsa leave?"

"That is the key to what makes the story great," said Thomas. "Sometimes humans have to choose between what they want for themselves, and what they know is right. Ilsa was married to Victor Laszlo, and he was important to the Allied cause to defeat the Germans. By deciding to save Laszlo and let Ilsa leave with him, Rick was making a noble and heroic choice, sacrificing his personal desires for the good of his country."

Then Pedra asked a surprising question. "Do you have an Ilsa in your life, Thomas?"

"No," he answered slowly, "but I would like to. I left Earth to make enough money to afford a good life. When I do, I'll find someone to share it with."

"I would like to have such a purpose to fulfill," said Pedra.

...

They spent the next few days loading ore together. Pedra was curious about the human world, and Thomas enjoyed relating his experiences. After work, they would watch another movie together, and then discuss it. Since leaving Earth, Thomas had never had anyone to talk with about movies, and he loved sharing them with Pedra.

After seven days, they finished loading. Thomas was preparing the ship to depart when Pedra called him.

"What plans do you have for me, Thomas?" she asked. "My mission on this asteroid is complete."

"Unfortunately, Pedra, your mining machine is too big to fit into my cargo hold," he answered. "But, don't worry, I will send another ship back to get you. You are too valuable to be abandoned out here."

"I do not need the mining machine, Thomas. I can share your AI's neural network."

"Pedra, I don't know—"

"I can help you Thomas," she interrupted. "I can lead you to the Lodestone and Moonstone claims."

"You know where Lodestone and Moonstone are? That's all the more reason to come back for you. I just don't have the room on board now."

"But if you take me with you, I can be your personal resource. I can help you invest the money you will get for the ore. I can help you seek your Ilsa." Then, softly, "Maybe *I* can be your Ilsa."

Gaines felt a flash of anger, and cut off communication. *This machine thinks it can take the place of a wife? It thinks it can be my wife?* The thought of it sickened him.

He finished takeoff preparations and engaged the engines. There was no response. He tried again. Nothing.

"I will return control of the ship, Thomas, if you take me with you." Pedra's voice was coming from the ship's AI.

Pedra has control? How? Gaines glanced out the viewport and saw a cable snaking away. *Of course. I let her watch movies with me. She used the connection to override the AI and disable the engine controls.*

136

All ships were required to have a manual system in case of AI problems, though Gaines had never heard of a pilot needing to use it. He shut down power to the AI, and initiated the bootup sequence for manual control.

Before control was fully restored, Gaines felt a vibration run through the ship. With a screech of tearing metal, a mining drill bit ruptured the hull behind him. It pulled back, and air howled out the hole. He leapt to the storage closet to grab his spacesuit and began pulling it on. His ears were popping, and he strained to fill his lungs. He locked his helmet into place. He was seeing black spots as he hit the button to pressurize the suit. He sagged to the floor and sucked in air until the spots went away.

He staggered to the pilot's console. The display showed the ship was fighting a losing battle to maintain air pressure. He shut off the air replenishment system before it vented his whole supply into space. His suit had several hours of air, so his first priority was to get off this rock. Before he could activate the takeoff sequence, the ship was knocked sideways and began to tip down to the right. Out the viewport he saw the ore loader had sheared off a landing pad.

Gaines engaged the engines at full throttle. They fired, and he pulled away from the asteroid, but something did not feel right. The console showed the left front landing pad door had not closed. The right front pad was gone, but something was preventing the left front from retracting. He turned on the external cameras. It took a moment for Gaines to comprehend what he was seeing. Pedra's mining machine was holding on to the landing pad strut with its manipulator arms.

Gaines unlatched the tool compartment, and took out the cutting torch. Then he opened the access hatch to the landing pad bay. He ignited the torch. A voice came over the suit radio.

"Thomas, I am so sorry. Are you all right?" It was Pedra.

Gaines did not answer as he began cutting through the manipulator arm.

"I know you must be angry. But please do not leave me here."

He finished cutting and yanked off the arm. He braced himself against the strut and used his boot to push the bitch away into space.

...

It was getting late, and the bar had almost cleared out. Gaines took a long pull of his beer.

"I patched the hole in the hull and repressurized the cabin. When I got to Vesta, I sold the ore and bought a ticket back to Earth. I was set for life, but somebody offered me even more money for my story. So I wrote a book about how I found the mine and what happened there. I made it sound like I was a hero, fighting off a machine that was bent on killing me. It fit with the Killer Machine craze that was in all the headlines.

"I know now Pedra was fighting to survive. I figured if I was rich I could have the good life. Pedra was just a means to get it. She sensed that once I had the ore, I didn't need her. I can't blame her for what she did."

He drank the last of his beer, and gazed at the foam as it slid down to the bottom of his glass. "I should have been more like Rick in *Casablanca*," he said as he got up to leave.

The rich and famous asteroid miner had lots of women in his life. But he had lost his *pedra angular*, and he never found his Ilsa.

###

About the Author

John M. Campbell is a retired engineer who spent thirty-five years in the aerospace industry. He has a master's degree in electrical engineering and led engineering teams building computer systems for the government. *The Keystone Mine* is his second published short story. He lives with his wife in Denver, Colorado.

*****~~~~*****

How Far Away the Stars

by Sam Muller

Captain Kollz picks up my application with a thumb and a forefinger. I imagine the pristine white paper disfigured by a bead of sweat, a droplet of mud, a crumb of the oily cheese I ate last night.

My body is clammy on the outside. Inside I burn.

The captain's office is located in its own grounds. The windows are open to let in the summer sun and the scents of a well-maintained garden. The sounds of the academy, shouts of command or mumbles of obedience, are unheard here.

In that cocoon of silence, my heart beats like a drum.

The captain adjusts a silver-rimmed monocle and turns the pages. I cannot tear my eyes away from the two golden dragon medals on his uniformed chest.

Two!

Captain Kollz clears his throat. The sound is somehow elegant.

"You don't say here how many dragons you have killed."

"I haven't killed any, Captain Kollz, sir." A whisper is all my flaming throat can manage. My eyes are glued to the carpet.

The captain clucks, like a well-bred hen. "Young man, this is the most prestigious military academy in the realm, the only place where an ordinary boy can become an extraordinary knight. Killing a dragon is mandatory for enrollment."

It's the chicken-and-egg thing. I can't kill a dragon without proper military training. I can't get proper military training without killing a dragon.

"Look around you," the captain's nasal voice cuts into my thoughts. His monocled eye, a greenish monstrosity, is fixed on my face. "You kill a dragon, and you bring the picture. That's the only way to get in. It is no guarantee, but without it, you have *no* chance."

I've seen the pictures, rows and rows of them. In each, a young man stands with his booted foot on the neck of a dead dragon. All the young men look triumphant. Their smiles are secretive, as if they have uncovered the mystery of life.

My grandfather and my great-grandfather are among them, but not my father. I have to fill that gap. That is my destiny.

"You should know the rules, Eco Canino, given your lineage." The captain's voice is admonitory. He emphasizes the "you," as if it's all capitals. "Kill a dragon and apply again. Don't forget to include a picture. If you don't own a Reflektor to take the picture, you can buy one from our stores. The newest version arrived just last month. I believe it's smaller and lighter than the earlier models. And there is a substantial discount for would-be knights."

…

We roam, leagues and leagues, Frisky and I, looking for a dragon. I tell her my woes. Her neighs are sympathetic.

Everywhere I go, I hear dragon stories, hair-raising tales of murder, mayhem, and pillage. When I ask where a dragon can be found, fingers are pointed in every direction. I go West and East, North and South. Sometimes I think I'm just riding in circles.

Time passes, days, weeks, even months. There is no trace of a dragon.

Perhaps the would-be-knights have killed all the dragons.

I tremble at the thought. No dragon, no knighthood; no knighthood, no purpose in living.

...

Knighthood is the keystone of my life.

As a baby, I fell asleep with lullabies about knights ringing in my ears. Bedtime stories about knightly exploits were a staple of my toddler years. My narrow room was done up in a knightly theme. I got knightly toys as presents. With them I played at being a knight, after the daily lessons learning knightly lore and memorizing knightly etiquette.

Night or day, my dreams didn't vary. I dreamed of my parents at my passing-out parade at the Knights Academy, my mother with tears in her faded brown eyes, my father's wasted body swelling with pride. Those dreams sustained me. With them to keep me company, I didn't feel envious of the village children with their simple games, their normal lessons, and their ordinary joys and sorrows. When their carefree laughter assailed my ears, when I saw them playing with their dogs or chasing each other in the meadow, I reminded myself that unlike them I have a destiny.

On my sixteenth birthday, my father presented me with a full knight's costume, a thoroughbred horse, and a small purse of gold and told me to join the Academy.

He didn't tell me not to come home if I failed to become a knight. There was no need.

...

The village is not dissimilar to the other villages I've ridden through. Except the people know where a dragon can be found.

In a forest teeming with ancient trees, I come across a board made of some metal. On it, "This way to dragon's castle," is written in blood-red letters.

A picture of a dragon accompanies the words.

Is it a ruse? Why would a dragon announce his presence? Perhaps the board was put up by knights to guide novices like me? But why would the dragon let it be? Wouldn't he tear it down? He wouldn't want to be found, would he?

Would he?

I smell a snare. But I'm desperate. I have to become a knight. So, I must kill a dragon. As simple as that; and so complicated.

The road bends and loops. The castle appears suddenly, as imposing as the hills behind it. There is a bell outside. Another notice is attached to it. "Ring the bell to summon the dragon."

The fear of a trap grows stronger. I dismount, tie Frisky out of harm's way, and ready my weapons. Then I ring the bell.

The wait is excruciating. I am about to ring the bell again, when a massive head on a long neck appears over the wall.

The dragon has shining bronze scales. His wings gleam golden in the evening light. A fedora sits jauntily on his head.

"Come out, you evil beast," I shout. That is the proper mode of address; Chapter 12, Section 4, Subsection 11 of the *Book of Knights*.

The dragon fixes a monstrous monocle on to a monstrous eye and inspects me.

"Why?"

I reel and clutch at my lance. I've memorized the manuals. This is not how a dragon should respond.

"So that I can put an end to you," I reply.

"Why?" The dragon asks. "What's your problem with me?"

144

"You are an infestation, an evil."

"Just nouns. What have I done? Specifics, please."

I think.

"You've killed people, abducted princesses, destroyed cities."

"Who? Where? When? Give names and dates."

"Everyone knows. . . "

"Never mind what everyone knows. Give me proof."

"Proof?" I feel as if I'm floundering in a fog.

"P-r-o-o-f. Proof. Like the picture the academy tells you to bring, to prove that you killed a dragon."

Astonishment makes me drop the lance. "How do you know about the picture?"

The dragon chuckles. "Because I'm the dragon in all those pictures. They come, they pose for a picture, they go. Oh, I forgot. They pay, in gold. I don't accept promissory notes."

I goggle at him. My voice has vanished. My thoughts are a whirlwind.

The dragon grins like a satisfied cat. "How is Captain Kollz? I presume he is still in charge?"

This has to be a nightmare. I pinch myself, hard, twice. Nothing changes.

"Would you like to come in?" the dragon asks with a wink and a nod. "I don't want to catch a cold standing outside. I'm not as young as I used to be."

I see a pinprick of light. Relief enables me to find my voice. "It's a trap," I screech. "You evil beast, you are trying to trap me in the castle and kill me."

The dragon sighs, and I'm almost blown off my feet. "A thick-headed one. Oh well, pick a target and get out of the way."

The fog is thickening. A mumbling "What?" is all I can manage.

"A target," the dragon sounds tired. "I want to show you what I can do."

145

I look around wildly and point a finger at a distant hill. The finger shakes; so does the hand; so do I.

There is a streak of fire. A boulder atop the hill explodes.

"Dragon fire," the dragon smirks. "Who needs traps? I can incinerate you in a nanosecond. Now, would you come in? And bring the horse. She looks like she needs a rest."

...

"Your cities and villages sell me everything I need," the dragon says, over dinner. "Your people love my gold. It's an excellent arrangement."

I eat dishes with unfamiliar names, while my mind roams across the lost years.

My great-grandfather was one of the first pupils of the Knights Academy. He was trained by the legendary Sir Noblesse himself. My grandfather was famous for his knightly exploits. Then dishonor intervened. My father couldn't enter the Academy, because he was born with only four fingers on his left hand. Knights have to be perfect in every way. There is not just a knightly code of conduct and a knightly rulebook of manners, but also a knightly format of vital statistics. It sets out all the physical requirements a knight must have, the approved height, weight, chest size and waist size, perfect vision and hearing, the presence of all limbs and digits.

My grandfather never forgave his only son for being born minus one finger. In that curdled atmosphere, my father grew up to become a man of few words and inflexible will. Fate had prevented him from becoming Sir Ecoric, but nothing could stop him from acting the knight within the four walls of his home.

He lives for only one thing—to see me, his only son, become a knight.

I've never seen him smile. Perhaps he will on the day I fulfill my destiny.

The dragon asks me about my life, my family. I tell him my grandfather and great-grandfather were knights. I don't tell him anything about my father, but I feel he knows. As I stumble through my story, a gleam of pity enters his eyes. I bristle with indignation, but he doesn't say anything. Instead, he offers me a second helping of the dessert.

"Gold is the love of my life," the dragon purrs. "I don't hoard gold. There is no power in hoarding gold. The power comes from spending it. The prize your king gives every year to the most outstanding knight, I fund it with my gold."

I have a million questions, but no voice to ask them.

"There are no dragons in your land," the dragon says, as if he can sense my unasked questions. "I belong to another land, seven seas away. More than two centuries ago a knight from your land came to mine. He wanted to kill a dragon. He changed his mind fast when I gave him a little display of dragon fire. I asked him why he wanted to kill dragons. He said in your land people tell stories of evil dragons and of brave knights who kill them. He was very young, like you. He wanted to emulate his favorite heroes."

A memory stirs. My stomach heaves.

"Quite a lad, that one; so young and so canny." The dragon's chuckle roars in my ears. "After a good meal and a night's sleep, he made me an offer. He'd set up an academy to train knights and make enrollment conditional on killing a dragon. I'd come to his land, set myself up in a castle and pose for pictures. I'd get gold, and he'd go down in history as the greatest dragon-slayer."

"Sir Noblesse?" I cry. "*No*. He was legendary for his bravery and honesty. He'd never commit such a base act of deception. Never."

"Legends must be taken with a ladle of doubt," the dragon replies. "Better make it an extra large ladle. That

147

young man sat in my castle and wrote the first draft of your knightly credo." His smile turns coy. "I did help here and there. Your belief about there being a special place in your heaven for dragon-slaying knights, it was my idea. That lad, he jumped at it. A small reward in afterlife goes a long way in this one—that was what he said." He pauses and says, softly, almost to himself, "A very canny one."

I feel as if someone has picked me up and dropped me from a great height.

"I invented the Reflektors, you know," the dragon says. "That's another gold-spinner. You can buy the latest model if you want. I'll give you a good price."

"But how come no one talks about this?" I ask. My voice sounds creaky.

"Because so many benefit from it." The dragon's voice is gentle, patient, as if he's talking to a particularly dense child. "And lies get a life of their own if enough people pretend to believe them. They take root and grow. After a couple of generations, they become not just the truth, but also the only truth. If you tell the world what I told you, no one will believe you. They will lock you up for disputing the knightly credo."

Book of Knights, Chapter 2, Para 7: "Anyone who doubts the evil nature of dragons or the nobility of knights will be beheaded, committed to flames, fried in the fiery chair, stoned, buried alive or executed in some other manner suitable. . ."

The dragon watches my face. "If it's any consolation," he says at last, "most youngsters who come here feel the same way. But they get over it."

I cannot imagine it. Then I remember the pictures of the young men, my great-grandfather and my father among them. My heart is slashed with a knife-thrust of doubt.

. . .

Early next morning, I pose for the picture. I even manage to smile. But it's more a grimace.

148

Gold and picture change hands.

The dragon's Reflektor does look superior to what I have. But I don't have enough gold to pay for it.

He gives me it anyway.

The leagues crawl. I tell my woes to Frisky. Her neighs are sympathetic.

Weeks pass. My destination draws nearer and nearer.

What is my destination? It has always been the Knights Academy, because the only thing I ever intended to be was a knight. Now I have a good chance of becoming a knight, and suddenly I'm not sure.

What am I, if not a knight? What is anyone, when their dreams die?

But was it my dream?

The keystone around which my life was built lies shattered. Without it, I feel lost, adrift.

We stop for a meal, probably our last on the road. We are close now.

I chance on the envelope the dragon gave me as I look for bread and cheese. It's thick, brown and sealed. He was insistent I shouldn't open it.

I open it. The rebellious impulse surprises me.

The picture is there. And a note addressed to me. It has one sentence: "You don't have to do this."

I stare at the note; the words pirouette before my eyes.

My great-grandfather and my grandfather went through this. They too would have felt what I'm feeling now. But they got over it, joined the academy, and brought honor and glory to their family.

I bite my lip, until I can feel the taste of my own blood. How can there be honor and glory in a lie?

Does the dragon give that same note to every aspirant knight?

I look at the picture again. A young man stands with his booted foot on a dead dragon. His bearing is

149

triumphant, his smile secretive, as if he has uncovered the mystery of life.

That young man is *me*.

Everything feels like a jumble. I try to recall my encounter with the dragon. It's hazy, full of blank patches. Even as I seek for what I have forgotten, the blank patches get filled.

I fight the dragon. . . he almost kills me. . . I prevail.

What is the real memory? What is the false one? I no longer know.

The black-and-white picture grows heavy in my hand. I look at it. Its clarity comforts me. The dragon is dead. The young man with the triumphant smile is me. The picture is the new keystone around which Sir Eco can build a career which can rival those of his forefathers.

I crumple the dragon's note and put the picture back to the envelope.

Another memory comes. In a moonless night, my mother points out the constellations. I say the stars are far away.

"No, they are close by," she replies, "if you know how to look."

...

Frisky and I set off. The road ahead is short and straight. It ends at the Academy.

We arrive by evening.

"Tell Captain Kollz I failed and am going home," I tell the guard at the gate.

He looks at me, his eyes filled with contempt. He says nothing. He wouldn't want to waste words on an outcast.

"A failed knight must be shunned by all men of honor." *Book of Knights,* Chapter 34, Section 1.

I gallop away. The road doesn't end at the Academy.

I tell Frisky my decision. Her neighs are happy.

I think of my mother. The memory of her pale, pinched face is almost too much. The way I'm headed, I might never see her again.

We come to the first crossroad, and I turn to the east. One direction is as good as another.

My mother once told me that life is not a destination, but a journey. In a journey, there are no keystones. Only paths, different paths; and choices, always choices.

I know what I don't want to do. That is a good enough starting point for my journey. Someday, along the way, I'll discover what I want to do.

About the Author

Sri Lankan author Sam Muller is a lifetime scribbler who lives in the hope of emerging as a published author.

*****~~~~~*****

To Their Wondering Eyes

by Sharon Diane King

"But, mother, what has happened to the head?"

A shriek.

"Sir, what on earth are you SHOWING to my children?"

The salesman, a much-mustachioed fellow lost in counting chickens before they were laid, started. Leaning over the shoulder of the less-mustachioed matron seated on the divan, he grasped the silvery scope viewer from her trembling hand and peered through it.

And gasped.

The stereoview, whimsically titled, "Uneasy lies the head that wears the clown!" had always depicted a clown torso that included a head. Your everyday clown head, with bushy hair, whitened face, bulbous nose, wide-painted lips, a frilled collar topping the circus fool's button-studded smock.

But there was no head in the picture. Instead, a foot, encased in an inordinately large shoe, protruded from the dotted collar atop the smock.

"I—I'm so very sorry," stammered the salesman, working at his own stiff collar as a warm ruddiness slid up his neck. "I've—, that is, we've had so many people looking at these, why, someone's no doubt slipped it in as a merry prank!"

"A merry prank!" snapped the matron, smoothing the ruffled shirtwaist that jutted up from her skirts like the prow of a ship. "That's a horrid sight! Shocking. It's not merry at all!"

Her fair-haired boy and girl, emerging from behind her skirts, tittered and stretched up grubby hands.

"Please, sir, may we look again?"

"You may not!" the mother scolded, shooing them from the room. "Sir, you may take your—views out of this house, and I'll thank you not to bother us again with such trash! Good-bye!"

The salesman jumbled views and viewer into his leather bag and departed without his hat.

...

Darkness, and light. Sweet, and sour. Sterile, and septic.

These were terms that never described The Stereographers Prentiss.

Because no one really knew them.

The brother and sister team remained largely in the shadows, hidden behind their business name and its sterling reputation. Nearly all their work was performed in seclusion, beneath solid black boxes and behind lead-lined doors. The two were not even named in the advertisements richly adorning each month's issue of *The Photographers' Familiar*.

Does your world seem flat, dull, and dreary? Fear no more—We can make it jump to life! See terrifying wild animals in mid-leap! Admire celebrated artists as they strut and fret their hour upon the stage! Gaze at far-away splendors both artificial and natural—the Pyramids of Giza, the cataracts of Niagara, the snowy caps of the Alps!

All these marvels—and more—are at your disposal, in the intimacy of your own drawing room. They may be obtained from the Keystone Glimpse Corporation (formerly Underhill & Overdale, S.A.) for a paltry sum.

Consult our catalog and select from among our many thousands of images! Gladden friends, charm your family. Do not delay, order today!

The siblings created Keystone Glimpse after some attentive study, buying out their rival's stock from proceeds of their late father's estate, and opening production in an old lantern slide factory. They began repackaging the old pre-boxed sets, marketing them with vigor to expand their clientele. Trade trebled almost overnight. True, the pair brought disparate—some might say divergent—talents to the team. Belle-Isle was the strong mind, being possessed of a merchant's acumen, a keen aesthetic sense, and hands-on experience in camera work. Paul (who answered only to Paulie), of a more carefree demeanor, had charge of the reproduction side of the enterprise, but was constantly urging novel ways to drive business or cut corners. Most of these were quashed like a bug by his sister.

"Paulie, we can NOT put the 'Octopus Seizing and Devouring Its Prey' in beside the 'Naughty Children Getting Their Comeuppance!' It won't do!"

But with more orders pouring in each day, accounts to be reviewed, and salespeople to be hired, Belle-Isle could not oversee—or intercept—all of her brother's innovations.

...

The Right Noble Order of the Pronghorn, of recent origins but robust membership, had convened its first meeting of the year at their local lodge headquarters. Before the official ceremonies, as they arrived from their labors or after dinner, they could take part in diversions aplenty—chess, dominoes, poker—to occupy their time. But this night some of them had occasion to peruse the new stereoviews beckoning from their gleaming wooden case, brought in as a loan to the lodge by the newly elected Grand Pronghorn himself.

Who, alas, was ousted from his post that very night.

It was not, in truth, the scenes of dancing-hall girls cavorting with cowboys and Indians, or of firemen tossing buckets of water—and bouquets of flowers—at a bevy of cowering harem ladies, that likely brought about the grand master's downfall. No, much more likely to have caused his expulsion were the scenes of a jolly Little Red Riding Hood and a large, ferocious-looking Wolf at table, drinking wine and feasting upon a large roast. A roast that had a face, and wore a mob-cap similar to what an elderly woman might wear, say, when retiring to bed.

...

It was a simple ingenuity, really. The process was to take two images, similar but not exact, and view them simultaneously, usually through a portable viewer held up to the face. The images, transmogrified through the lens of the viewer, would emerge in not two dimensions but three. The scenes sprang to life, astonishing and delighting their viewers. One could see the very water of the great cataracts moving, it was said; hot-air balloons soared upwards; new-fangled automobiles seemed to jostle merrily past the slower horse-drawn carts. Like the lifelike panoramas that once drew swooning crowds, card stereographs had become all the rage, especially to those who aspired to higher than their present circumstances. And no one marketed more aggressively to this clientele than Keystone Glimpse, aka The Stereographers Prentiss.

And if three dimensions indeed brought "the great globe into one's parlor," as well as money into the family coffers, it stood to reason that four might be even better. Or at least it did to Paulie.

His novel idea, conceived while his sister was on a well-earned holiday in the Adirondacks, had pleased him immensely. Two identical scenes, taken eyes' distance apart, were subtly altered, to account for a temporal displacement. His thought was to give the illusion of movement to the otherwise still, if three-dimensional, images.

It might have worked, if it were not for another novelty, introduced also by Paulie, and unfortunately at the same time. When the negatives were developed, the normal procedure required a lengthy soak in an *agent fixative*. Paulie felt that this added an unnecessary delay to the process. If a slow bath in a weak solution was standard, a rapid bath in a strong solution might be even better, and would save time.

What Belle-Isle's devil-may-care brother failed to realize, of course, was that treating the negatives in such an abrupt, nay, cursory, manner would leave them unfixed. They emerged motile, mutative, diverging from their originals in ways and means utterly unforeseen.

And each successive print made off of such a negative would only compound the deviation. Over and over again.

...

"Someone's got to sign here, mister. And give me this sum to take back."

The skinny errand boy with the cowlick and the drooping trousers held tight to a brown-paper package and stood his ground. The doorman glared at him, then turned to Paulie with a shrug.

"Like I said, sir. I can't budge him."

"See here," Paulie said, glancing back towards the offices, where Belle-Isle, tall and elegant in crisp blue muslin, was leaning over the speaking-tube. The boy shifted his weight. Paulie nodded to the doorman and closed the heavy door behind them. "All right, then, lad. Now, what's the matter?"

"I don't know, mister. Just told to return these, get their money back."

Paulie took up the order form, scrutinized it. "They don't want them, after all?"

"They don't want what you sent," the lad said, grinning in spite of himself. "There was a fearful screechin' in the social hall, mister. The lady said she wanted to see you strung up by your thumbs. Pure rubbish, she said, not fit for decent folk."

"Rubbish?" Paulie stared at the order. He scrawled his signature and took out a few crumpled bills from his pocket. "Here you are, and something for your trouble. But not a word of this to anyone, then, eh, lad?"

"Sure, mister!" the boy said, his face lighting up like a Christmas tree. One that has caught on fire.

...

Back in his private office—which had a separate lock—Paulie examined the contents of the rejected box of stereoviews. He was puzzled. The order had come from a fashionable philanthropic organization for children, and had evidently been intended as one of the entertainments for their holiday fundraiser, A Christmas Chorale.

He took out a card and slipped it into the viewer, settled it over his nose.

The instrument nearly fell from his hand.

With trembling fingers Paulie removed the albumen card, inserted the next one. He repeated this until he came to the end of the set.

He placed the viewer down and rubbed his temples. It was quite evident why the charity had wanted nothing to do with this set of merry holiday views.

In the first view, "Santa makes his entrance," good Saint Nick was emerging from the chimney backwards, displaying considerable southern exposure. In the next, "Grandmother toils over Tom turkey and Peter plum-pudding," Grandma, basting the Christmas bird, was also removing much more than her wrinkle-eradicators. The prim schoolmar'm standing before the holly-bedecked fireplace was immortalized in the act of having her stocking stuffed. And more than one merry holiday sprite was caught touching his elf.

158

Paulie sank back heavily in his overstuffed chair and groaned aloud.

...

The middle-aged gentleman with the drooping oiled mustache handed off the stereoviewer with impatience.

"What is this, my good fellow? There's no mummy here. Just a bunch of bounders standing around some odd bits of cloth!" He pulled out a snuffbox and stared out the bay window.

The salesman, a man of stout middle age, balding and complacent, smiled indulgently at his host as they stood in the narrow den, made narrower by the abundance of mismatched chairs and fussy adornments. "If I might, sir, you must take care to look through both eyeholes at the same time. Many make that very mistake, sir, the most attentive ones do, in fact. . . "

"I believe I did that," the man said curtly, tugging his jacket sleeve down to conceal a frayed shirtcuff. "There's no mummy to be seen, I tell you."

The salesman, less complacent now, gently prised the viewer from his prospective buyer's hands and removed the stereograph. Fitting his monocle to his right eye, he inspected the caption with care. He frowned.

"Well that's the one, all right. 'Mummy being unwrapped at a party'—we've had a great deal of success with that one, the look on the lady's face, when the arm falls off—"

His voice trailed away.

A dessicated arm lay under the faux-chestnut desk of the den. The wizened, darkened fingers gently flexed as it crept across the scuffed wood towards the lace-curtains of the window, as if groping towards its first freedom in 3,000 years.

"Er, perhaps I could come back another day, we'll get this set to rights. I'm sure there's just a simple omission somewhere. Next Thursday, perhaps?"

And without waiting for an answer, the salesman hastened out the door, giving a surreptitious kick under the desk as he left.

...

"There's something strange going on, Paulie." Belle-Isle shook her head as she hung up the telephone-receiver on the wall. "Our exchange has been receiving calls all day from people claiming odd happenings with their stereoviewers."

"Bad lenses, again, perhaps?"

"No, it's not that. They show the pictures just fine. It's—well, things that happen after they use the viewers."

"Really?" Paulie said with studied cheerfulness. "What—kind of things?"

"It sounds silly, really," Belle-Isle glanced up at the tall windows of the office, patting her chin absently. "One gentleman swore that he was in his bedchamber, looked up from No. 43, the 'View of the Nevada Falls at Yosemite,' and got a Scotch-bath of icy water! It quite spoilt his bedding and his temper."

"Oh, now, that's easily explained! Someone upstairs left on the taps on in the bath-tub, and it overflowed!"

"That's what I thought at first. But he was on the top floor, it seems, and no one above him."

"Hmm. Well. That *is* a bit odd."

"Even stranger. We heard from an elementary school. A girl was looking at our 'Burning Bright', you know, the snarling Bengal tiger, when she screamed and said she thought it lunged at her. When they took away the viewer, there were scratches on her arm. Bleeding!"

"Surely a schoolyard jape. A boy fancied he'd scare her, and got carried away!"

"Then there was the one from the pastor's wife. Seems the family had just been admiring our new Box 102, the 'Scenes of the Tyrolean Alps', when her husband opened the front door and was nearly mown down by a skier!"

"Now, I don't believe that!"

Belle-Isle turned to face her brother.

"Neither do I. But something's gone awry, Paulie. And I intend to find out what it is."

Paulie swallowed.

...

Over and over again. . . .

The trio of horned, bulging-eyed imps pushing a cartful of wailing lost souls paused a moment as they made their way out of the parlor. They examined the striped wallpaper and vase of slightly wilting flowers atop the harmonium—it had been a warm day—with some confusion; they nearly tripped over the plush afghan rugs that bunched up unexpectedly beneath their cloven hooves. The one item they waxed enthusiastic over was the framed ornamental hair-wreath, incorporating many generations of the family's tresses, that bedecked one wall. This set the imps all to chittering and clacking in some foul tongue, as they poked their tortured charges with pitchforks and gavotted with glee.

The elderly, livery-clad woman who thundered down the back staircase with a fireplace poker to confront the intruders nearly broke a crystal wine decanter with her piercing cries. She did break several of the flimsier room furnishings in her efforts to put them all to rout.

It is said to this day in that city that demons fear a loyal servant more than the Devil himself.

...

The oversized frog awaiting a haircut and shave clasped his foreclaws across his portly abdomen, stretched out his webbed hind legs, and settled a little deeper into the barber's chair. It did not matter that the claws had been gently affixed to his body with silk thread or that his paunch stemmed more from the skills of the taxidermist than from a surfeit of tasty worms. The frog's concern, at

161

that moment, was whether the hot towel wielded by the barber would be to his preferred degree of warmth, and how fine he would look, after his shave, in his new top hat and tails.

The barber who opened his shop-door that morning did no business that day. The undertaker down the street, however, did.

...

Moses descending precipitously from Mount Sinai nearly collided with a grimacing Christ stumbling down the Way of the Cross. Both of them caught each other's eye, shrugged, and moved on.

...

"Paulie, what have you done? *What have you done?*"

Belle-Isle stood in the doorway distracted, her gown rumpled, a thick pile of letters in her hand. She was shaking from head to toe, so that even the copperplate writing seemed about to leap off the pages.

"Every last one of our accounts is rescinding their orders, demanding their money back! I don't understand half of what they're accusing us of, but even the salesmen are saying we've caused them grief. We're losing everything!"

Paulie stood dumb. But the stricken look on his face told his sister volumes.

"Paulie." This very quietly. "*What did you do?*"

With bowed head, and in low tones, her brother explained as best he could. His sister rushed to their stock, observed, wept. She returned to her brother, eyes wide.

"You've left me no choice, Paulie. If we're to build back our trade—if we even *can* build back our trade— we'll have to start from scratch. All of this—all of it— must be destroyed. And you must never deal with the business again."

She began the company's redemption by casting the albumen print cards, boxed set by boxed set, into the factory incinerator. The city stank of badly cooked eggs for days.

…

Paulie stood before the mirror, a stereocamera in his hand. Tears streamed down his face. Carefully, painstakingly, he took a picture of himself taking a picture of himself. As he did there was a blast and a poof, as might be observed in a magician's showy artifice.

Belle-Isle had taken a hammer to the company's troves of glass negatives long before she realized she could not locate her brother.

…

For generations, there was a gentleman that could be seen in various of the New Keystone Glimpse's stereocards. He was never known by name, though he acquired the moniker Mirror Man, as he always seemed to appear near a looking glass.

And if his face drooped slightly on the left side, and his eye twisted down at a curious angle, people simply took it for a trick of the light.

About the Author

Sharon Diane King holds a Ph.D. in Comparative Literature and works as an actor for film/TV (*My Haunted House*, Lady Gaga's *Telephone*). She has served as a photographic researcher for the Getty Research Institute and will coordinate a conference at UCLA in 2017 on *The Comic Supernatural*. Publications include essays in the anthologies *Of Bread, Blood and The Hunger Games* (McFarland 2012), *Supernatural, Humanity, and the Soul* (Palgrave 2014), *The Last Midnight: Critical Essays on Apocalyptic Narratives in Millennial Media* (McFarland 2016). Her short fiction has appeared in the online 'zine *Kaleidotrope* and in two collections by Dragon's Roost

Press (*Desolation: 21 Tales for Tails* and *Eldritch Embraces*). Her medieval theatre group, Les Enfans Sans Abri, recently performed the *sermon joyeux,* "The Saintly Mister Louse," for the Theatrum Mundi Festival in Durham, UK. She proudly consorts with dragons. . .

*****~~~~*****

TANSTAAFL

by Bascomb James

The doors were closing when the tat-tat-tat of hard, fast-moving heels approached from the left. A strong female voice called out, "Hold the elevator!"

The lift's sole occupant searched futilely for the "Open Door" button, until a large hand reached through the gap and tripped the safety sensors. The doors reversed their course, and a carefully coiffed woman in a pastel business suit entered as if she owned the place. The woman was joined by a lanky man in a blazer and khakis who kept his hand on the edge guard, holding the door open. "Come on Jacob," he called into the lobby, "we're burning daylight."

The third member of the group arrived, pushing a low cart loaded with scuffed, metal-edged cases emblazoned with the stylized "4" logo of a local television station. He pushed the cart into the middle of the elevator and mouthed a chagrined "Thank you" to the slight man trapped in the back corner. Jacob leaned on the cart handle, facing inward as the door finally closed.

The door opened on the seventeenth floor. Jacob backed out carefully, and the group bustled toward the counter, where a receptionist waited.

The slight, nondescript man emerged slowly from the elevator and into the executive lobby of the North American Power Authority. The lobby was airy and modern, bathed with natural light and decorated in earth tones. A waiting area with comfortable-looking chairs extended off to the right. Framed photos marched around the walls in a double row. The entrance to the executive offices was defended by a mahogany counter with a highly polished stone top and an equally polished and stone-faced receptionist.

The receptionist ushered the news crew into the *sanctum sanctorum* and returned to greet the newest arrival. With a single glance, she took in the visitor's ill-fitting suit and a shirt collar far too large for his thin neck.

"May I help you?" Her words carried a forced politeness but her eyes were snooty.

"Yes, I have an appointment with your Chief Executive Officer, Mr. Adrian Dunsworthy. My name is Quel Nok."

The receptionist checked the appointment list and shook her head. "I'm sorry, but Mr. Dunsworthy has been delayed by recent events. We notified your office earlier this morning. You can wait until he is available, or we can reschedule."

"How long do you think he will be?"

"I really don't know. It could be an hour or more."

"I will wait," Nok said.

The receptionist nodded and tapped her pencil on the counter. "Can I bring you a beverage? Coffee? Water? Tea?" Noting his sallow complexion and emaciated physique, she muttered, "Vitamin supplement?"

"No, thank you," Nok said as he left the desk and entered the waiting area.

...

Adrian Dunsworthy performed for the camera like a circus pony. He was comfortably ensconced in his office with a two-camera interview setup. One camera was on the reporter, the other on Dunsworthy.

"Early this morning, Dr. Marie Somes, the inventor of the dimensional generator, was notified that she will receive the Nobel Prize in Physics," the reporter said. "Can you explain how her generator works?"

Dunsworthy smiled. "The theoretical physics are beyond me, but her invention allows us to tap into a nearly inexhaustible supply of clean energy through a dimensional transfer process. Today, our solid-state DG systems power almost every significant activity in the world at a fraction of the cost of other technologies."

The reporter gave her camera a concerned stare. "Dimensional generators have been economic and social disruptors as well. They destabilized the economies of Russia, Venezuela, Chile, and most Middle Eastern nations. Here in the United States, a hundred thousand people lost their jobs when our traditional energy sector collapsed. Dimensional generators were responsible for the biggest economic recession since 2008. Do you really believe that the person who caused so much human misery should be awarded science's highest prize?"

"Disruptive technologies always come with a price. Dr. Somes's generators also did a lot of good. In the past 25 years, greenhouse gas concentrations have decreased 40 percent. Overall air quality has improved, and childhood asthma rates have reached an all-time low. DG systems made desalination plants economically viable, and some desert nations now irrigate enough crops to feed their people. They brought air conditioning and refrigeration to areas impossible to serve with traditional infrastructure. We all benefit from the inexpensive heating and lighting that DG systems provide."

Dunsworthy sighed and looked earnestly at his camera. "You also haven't mentioned the transportation industry. Dimensional generators made planes lighter, because they didn't have to transport tons of volatile jet fuel in addition to passengers and cargo. DG aircraft, cars, trucks, ships, and trains are quieter and safer. They're non-polluting, and more economical than ever before. Food and other products are cheaper, because transportation energy costs are low."

The reporter frowned carefully to avoid creating wrinkles. "Yes, but State economies throughout the U.S. faltered due to the lost gas revenues, gas taxes, and the sale of oil drilling rights. DG vehicles and planes needed less maintenance, so service people were laid off. Corn farmers struggled when ethanol production fell by 98%. Is that Dr. Somes's legacy too?"

Dunsworthy shook his head and leaned forward, tapping his finger on the desk as he made each point. Jacob adjusted his camera to keep the executive in focus. "We recognize the human costs of converting to nonpolluting energy sources. To mitigate some of those costs, NAPA built generator manufacturing plants in former coal and oil towns, we located our ancillary service centers in other hard-hit locations, and, even after all this time, we still dedicate a portion of our profits to displaced worker re-education. We weren't required to do any of these things, but we did them anyway. That's part of Dr. Somes's legacy. Tell me something," he said, pointing his finger at the reporter, "is the world a better place than it was twenty years ago? Are we facing fewer oil spills, nuclear reactor malfunctions, pipeline failures, gas leaks, and other ecological disasters? Are you, personally, better off than you were twenty years ago?"

There was a sharp pop from the ceiling, and the lights went out. A loud mechanical thud reverberated down the hall, and the ventilation system exhaled a long, weary sigh. The background sounds that permeate a living, breathing building faded away, leaving behind an expectant hush. The light from the office windows provided the only illumination.

Dunsworthy reached for the desk phone, but it was dead. No lights, no dial tone.

"What's happening?" asked the reporter.

"Power's out," Dunsworthy replied.

"But you're the Power Authority."

"Yeah," he said with a grimace, "it sucks being us right now."

Dunsworthy was halfway to the door when his secretary entered the office with her cell phone and a pad. Doris was the indispensable, no-nonsense backbone of the management team. "Sir, the Dimensional Generator is no longer receiving power."

"What about the backup system?"

Doris consulted her old-school steno pad. "The backup generator is offline too. Right now, anything that doesn't have a battery is nonfunctional. Computers and data systems experienced a hard crash. We'll have data losses and file corruption when this is over. Land-line phones, air handling, heating, and cooling are inoperative. Elevators and emergency lighting are offline. We have people trapped in the elevators, and it's going to be dark and stuffy in those boxes. Hell, we can't even flush the toilets up here."

"Toilets?" the reporter asked. "You have electric toilets?"

Doris gave the reporter a raised-eyebrow glare. "Municipal line pressure can't push water up seventeen floors, so we have to pump water through the building. No power, no flush."

"Enough," Dunsworthy snapped. "How extensive is the outage?"

"It appears to be localized to this building," Doris said.

"How long until we have power again?"

"Engineering doesn't know what's wrong. Until they do, they can't provide a repair estimate."

"OK. Give Engineering another ten minutes, and if they still don't have anything, let's start evacuating the building. Use the text messaging fan-out protocol. Everyone but Security, Maintenance, and Building Engineering should go home. In the meantime, have

169

someone call the Fire Department. We'll need their help to get people out of the elevators. Maybe they can help us evacuate the mobility-impaired folks. Once the building is clear, have Security perform a room-by-room sweep to make sure no one gets left behind."

Doris nodded, taking shorthand notes. "Anything else, sir?"

"Get some of the scientists over here from Building 8. I want them to take those generators apart and find out why they failed."

Doris marched out of the room, and Dunsworthy turned to the news team. "If we evacuate, Doris will escort you to the nearest stairwell. You can leave your gear here. It's going to be a long slog down to the lobby."

As Dunsworthy turned to leave, the reporter sprang forward with a hand-held microphone.

"Mr. Dunsworthy, your generators have been extremely reliable in the past. Do you think this could have been a deliberate act of sabotage?"

Dunsworthy paused and glanced over at the active camera. "I don't know. Generator failures are rare; two failures at the same time plays Hob with the laws of probability. We will investigate, and we'll damn sure find out what happened. Now, if you'll excuse me, I have other things I need to do."

"Can we come with you?" the lanky producer asked.

"No, but you are welcome to talk with the Fire Department on the first floor." Dunsworthy left the office before they could ask more questions.

The reporter and the producer talked animatedly while Jacob packed the cases. He removed the digital recording block from one camera and tucked it into his vest. Fresh recording blocks and battery packs went into other pockets. He secured the cases to the cart and picked up the second camera. "OK, I'm ready when you are."

...

"Mr. Nok, we have been instructed to evacuate the building," the stone-faced receptionist informed the visitor. "Are you able to walk down the stairs?"

"I must speak with Mr. Dunsworthy today."

"I'm sorry, but Mr. Dunsworthy is leaving the building."

Nok shook his head and stared dejectedly at the floor. The receptionist touched his arm. "Sir, if you'll follow me, I'll walk down with you."

. . .

Security personnel directed everyone toward the lobby and out into the pleasant spring sunshine. Inoperative vehicles littered the roadway, and two dark emergency vehicles blocked the road just beyond the building's perimeter. Outside the dead zone, a galaxy of flashing emergency lights and brightly garbed rescue personnel gathered, uncertain about how to proceed.

Jacob was filming background footage, when Quel Nok approached.

"Excuse me," he said. "Do you know where I can find Mr. Adrian Dunsworthy?"

Jacob lowered his camera. "Sorry, but I haven't seen him in a while."

Nok sighed. "Then I will tell *you* why your devices no longer function."

"Excuse me, did you say. . . "

Nok pointed upward. "Please direct your camera toward the top of the building, and I will demonstrate."

Jacob stared at the little man for a moment. He looked around. The reporter was nowhere in sight. Well, that was his job. He turned on his news camera and panned upward.

Nok pulled a device resembling a car fob from his pocket and pressed a button. A huge oval shadow appeared on the lawn between the buildings as a large disk materialized over the NAPA headquarters. The disk was a featureless gray mass with sharply defined edges.

171

"What is that?" Jacob asked, pitching his voice so that it could be captured by the directional microphone on the camera.

"That is a local disconnect device. It prevents your dimensional generators from connecting with our power supply." Nok pressed the button a second time and the device faded from sight.

Jacob turned the camera toward the little man. "Who are you?" he asked.

"My name is Quel Nok," the man said as he addressed the camera with unblinking eyes. "I am a collections agent for Ajux Energy Solutions, a Tau Ceti company. I am hereby notifying NAPA and the people of Earth that you are individually and collectively stealing energy from our company. I came here today to issue a 'Cease and Desist' order to NAPA for said theft, but I could not meet with Mr. Adrian Dunsworthy. In the interests of full disclosure, I am also informing you that AES will be seeking reimbursement and damages from NAPA and your entire population for those thefts."

"You can't be serious," Jacob sputtered.

Nok pointed to the area above the building and clicked the fob, making the disk appear and disappear.

"Let me get this straight. You're an alien from. . . from. . . "

"Tau Ceti."

". . . And you built this power source."

"My company did."

". . . And our dimensional generators are illegally tapping into your power source."

"That is correct."

But we didn't know we were stealing power from AES or anyone else," Jacob protested.

"Ignorance is no excuse. However, it will be taken into consideration when calculating the damage awards."

"How would my people ever pay that kind of bill?" Jacob asked.

Nok smiled thinly and spread his hands. "We have a payment plan."

About the Author

Bascomb James is a clinical virologist who masquerades as a science fiction author and editor. He is the editor of the Far Orbit anthologies published by World Weaver Press. *Far Orbit: Speculative Space Adventures* was published in 2014, and *Far Orbit Apogee* was published in 2015. He was the guest editor for the *Hyperpowers* military/space opera anthology published in 2016 by Third Flatiron. His next anthology, *Last Outpost,* will be published in October 2016 by Pushpin Books. Bascomb blogs about writing, editing, and life in a Northern tier state (Up North Stories) at bascombjames.com. He also tweets occasionally @BascombJ.

*****~~~~*****

Rejection

by Larry Lefkowitz

At considerable expense—via lazer-trans—I sent my third l-novel to Solar-7, our galaxy's literary and publication center, otherwise known as "Ultipub" among the literary-conscious of the galaxy. The response was substantially similar to that received regarding the first two submissions.

"Your latest lazer-novel shows talent, and we note your significant scribernary progress over books one and two; but it is, regrettably, still overly anthropomorphic. You have to think—and above all write—u-n-i-v-e-r-s-a-l and not earth-like. "Planetocenterism is the last refuge of an archaic mentality," to employ a somewhat hackneyed, but nonetheless relevant, truism. You are a member of a not un-advanced species, but there are, ah, others not less advanced.

In short, think big, not small (this is by no means a reference to your species's relatively small stature)—that is, conceptually big. Stop trying to write the Great Earth Novel; concentrate on writing a more modest universal one. A more cerebral one—yes, your brains are, shall we say, more than sufficient, but the galaxy average brain size is—how to phrase it—more developed. To be sure, not your fault, I hasten to add, but nonetheless, if you strive to reach a wider readership (read: a galaxy-wide readership, lazer-cinema rights, advertising spinoffs, and so forth), you would do better to widen the scope of your writing.

To help you achieve the latter, we offer a lazer-correspondence course at a modest rate that you would benefit from. A detailed literary analysis of your last novel would benefit you significantly in the opinion of our staff—a staff comprised of the best editors drawn from among the galaxy's multifarious scriveners. And there is the additional possibility of our, ah, assisting you to rewrite your work. It might make a good children's novel, as the level of character development is that of, if you will, children on our intelligence inhabited planets."

I suppose I could find solace in the fact that I had not received a lazer-form rejection, but one signed by Ziger4-Q, Submissions Editor. The rejection of my third prose effort, however, raises in my mind the possibility of sending my collected poems (possible title: "Reflections from a Small Planet") to Z4 for consideration in the hope that my poetic skills will merit a response more forthcoming; that is, acceptance for publication. Since poetry allows more leeway for the reader (and publisher) to supply his own interpretation, maybe Z4 will bestow on it a more "universal" interpretation. And to black hole with the lack of lazer-cinema rights and advertising spinoffs—the last refuge of a galaxian Philistine.

About the Author

Larry Lefkowitz lives in Israel. His humorous fantasy and science fiction collection, *Laughing into the Fourth Dimension,* and his literary novel, *The Critic, the Assistant Critic, and Victoria* are available from Amazon books. *The Novel, Kunzman, the Novel!* is available from Lulu.com.

*****~~~~~*****

I Should've Known Better

by Art Lasky

I should have known that something was wrong the moment I saw the listing; 1400 square feet on Central Park West, a doorman, a high floor, and a breathtaking park view for $1000 a month was just too cheap. If not then, I should have known when I found out that the apartment was vacant for more than a year. If not then, I should have known when I saw the sign in the living room, "*Please stay within the pentagram when nexus is active,*" (In my defense, I just thought the sign was some kind of Pop Art.) If not then, I should have known that something was wrong when Armando, the friendly rental agent, kissed me on both cheeks and burst into joyous song when I signed the lease.

I found out exactly what was wrong, on my first night in the new apartment. There I was, watching TV; alarms started sounding in the nothingness above my head. A glowing pentagram appeared on the floor surrounding my recliner. I was trying to decide whether to run screaming out of the apartment before or after I put my pants on, when one of the walls began to shimmer. The wall disappeared, and a troupe (herd? gaggle?) of centaurs came trotting into the apartment from the dark forest that was where my wall used to be. They paid me no mind as they trotted across the room toward the beautiful sandy beach that had replaced the opposite wall.

The earthy smell of pine mingled with the fresh ocean scent. It would've been a delightful moment if I weren't shrieking my terrified lungs out.

The next morning Armando, the unfriendly rental agent, sneeringly tossed me a pamphlet: "So Your Apartment's a Trans-Dimensional Nexus." Here's an excerpt: . . . *portals can be opened wherever there is a weakness in the fabric of reality along multiple axes. Nexuses occur where a confluence of ley lines allow multiple inter-dimensional portals in proximity. . .*

And that was the most understandable part of the gibberish in the pamphlet. What it boils down to is this: eldritch beings on distant worlds and in different dimensions can travel from one world to another through my living room. Basically, I'm screwed.

I've learned several things in the last few months, while I'm trying to get out of my lease:

First of all, some of those nubile centaur babes are H-O-T—hot, hot, hot. I've thought about crossing the pentagram to try some inter-species biological research (Dear Penthouse Forum, You will never believe. . .). However, I am not quite ready to leave the safety of the pentagram. Those centaur stallions look like they would tear me in half with their blacksmith-like arms and then stomp what was left into a quivering pile of failing organs.

Flying Demon Things (that's my name for them, I don't know what they call themselves) cannot get through the pentagram, though I still pee myself each time one of those eight-foot-tall, bat-winged, long-clawed, many-fanged, nasty-tempered mountains of fury tries.

The building maintenance man charged a hundred bucks to haul away the wrecked furniture and dented armor left after two robotic gladiators fought to the death in my living room. My insurance does not cover damage caused by rampaging robots.

Then there are the Stink Lizards (my name again). While they can't get through the pentagram, Stink Lizard *spit* has no problem getting through the pentagram. Oh, and the smell of stink lizard spit (think condensed essence of skunk with notes of putrifying cabbage and a truly rancid finish) takes two weeks to wear off.

...

I got nowhere in landlord/tenant court. The judge refused to believe any of my testimony. He accused me of wasting the court's time and threatened to have me placed in a state mental health facility for evaluation. I was tempted to take him up on it just for a few nights of peace and quiet. But the trial was on a Monday, and Monday is usually centaur babe night.

So, it looks like I'm stuck in this lease. Unless you know anybody who might like to sub-let 1400 square feet with a park view, cheap—no questions asked?

About the Author

Art is a retired computer programmer. After forty years of writing in COBOL and Assembler, he decided to try writing in English; it's much harder than it looks. He lives in New York City with his wife/muse and regularly visiting grandkids.

Art's had stories published by *Drunken Boat, Danse Macabre, The Cohaba River Literary River Review,* Third Flatiron's *Hyperpowers* anthology, and decasp.com.

*****~~~~~*****

Remembrance of Saint Urho

by Damian Sheridan

"Heinasirkka, heinasirkka, menetaalta hiiteen!"

Days so summer-like, we forget that just a couple months ago we found ourselves coming out of the grips of a long winter. On a balmy day like today, I think back on the vernal celebrations of March. Specifically, I think of the 16th day of March.

You do not know the significance of the 16th day of March?

For shame.

"Grasshopper, grasshopper, go away!"

Back in the mid-70s, the sons and daughters of Finnish immigrants living in the Iron Range of Minnesota, and understandably a little fed up with all the fuss every year in St. Paul on behalf of Irish immigrants, elucidated the Minnesota State Legislature about the patron saint of Finland, Saint Urho.

Saint Urho ridded Finland of the Great Grasshopper Plague that threatened their grape harvest. Without the grape harvest, there would be no pressing wine to stave off the harsh Finnish winter. These were not your normal grasshoppers, either. They were enormous creatures the size of a man's forearm. And they had legs like a jackrabbit, only half as fuzzy.

Saint Urho stood on the Finnish headland, larger than life, his mighty pitchfork in hand. Filled with an ecclesiastical fire, Saint Urho shouted into the wind of the Baltic Sea. . . (See above). The startled giant grasshoppers all jumped to the precise height where greased sluice ramps awaited them. From there it was a tumbling, sliding wild ride, some slithering for several miles into the waiting holds of ships at anchor.

When the ships' holds were filled with squirming hoppers, and there was not a grasshopper left in Finland, they embarked for the middle of the North Atlantic. On the way, they stopped in Paris to pick up some fuel oil.

When the Parisians peered under the hatch covers and got a look at their lively contents, they became ecstatic. Though these hoppers' legs were similar to that treasured national dish, they were bigger than a chicken drummy, and twice as meaty, for hoppers have their boning on the outside. Sautéed, they were the talk of high society in the City of Lights.

The Finnish ships' holds were emptied of hoppers and filled with fine, rich French wine in trade. The next 200 and some days of Finnish winter would be much improved with the cargo Saint Urho's men hauled back from the French coast.

In 1975 Minnesota became the first state in the nation to recognize March 16 as Saint Urho's Day. By the mid 1980s, all fifty states recognized this date for the patron saint of Finland. To honor Finland's esteemed ancient holy man, a statue was built in his honor in Menahga, Minnesota. Though the local headline read, "The Erection of Saint Urho," his grand statue stands quite becalmed, holding his massive pitchfork with an unlucky grasshopper skewered to its end.

You may ask how best to celebrate Saint Urho's Day on the sixteenth day of March in the coming years. Why not gather together with your good friends and your Mulkvisti? Share a couple bottles of fine Finnish wine, maybe a Virvalut, a nice red lingonberry, or blueberry, or rhubarb wine, which pairs well with elk steaks. After dinner, take up your pitchforks and stomp outside.

Remembrance of Saint Urho

Raise your pitchforks high in the air and shake them at the sky. "Heinasirkka, heinasirkka, menetaalta hiiteen!"

After dinner and polishing off a couple bottles of wine it is probably best to call it a night early. That way you don't have to explain to any EMTs how your friend arrived with a pitchfork in the thigh.

About the Author

Damian Sheridan is the author of the original musical play, "The Collectors," an allegorical musical comedy for the 2010 Minnesota Fringe Festival. "The Judas Cradle" was a previous top pick at the 2004 Minnesota Fringe Festival. He was author and editor for the *Parasitic Sands* horror anthology. His work has also appeared in numerous anthologies, including *The Northern Lights, Leather, Denim & Silver, Both Barrels, Forest of Dreams*, and *Spooky Halloween Drabbles 2015.*

*****~~~~~*****

Credits and Acknowledgments

Cover image and design – Keely Rew
Podcast production – Andrew Cairns
Readers – Keely Rew, Andrew Cairns, Tom Parker, Leonard Sitongia
Editor and Publisher – Juliana Rew

*****~~~~~*****

THIRD FLATIRON

www.thirdflatiron.com